THERE WAS A GIRL ...

THERE WAS A GIRL ...

PANKAJ GUPTA

KALPAZ

ISBN : 978-93-8022-342-1

First Published, 2019

Published by

GenNext Publication
5, Ansari Road
Daryaganj, New Delhi-110002
Phone: 9811692060
E-mail: gennextpublication@hotmail.com

Printed at: G. Print Process, Delhi.

Dedicated to all whose progression of life changed due to various malpractices of our society, my mother and my Uncle Dr Subhash Gupta

Author's Note

"The most dangerous creation of any society is the man who has nothing to lose."

– James A Baldwin

India in spite of being a socially diverse country with various religions, castes, colours, cultures, festivals, languages, and cuisines that bring lots of diversity in our society. Still, this country is a great example of Unity in Diversity as it is the largest democracy in the world for the past so many decades. Many countries have restructured politically and their democratic structure has either left out far behind or it is just for namesake but here in India, it is very strong and sustained for last so many decades and getting stronger day by day. I feel this is the only achievement our leaders have and deserve a round of applause for keeping it intact barring a few months of the emergency.

Besides Democracy, what unites India is the cricket match as whenever there is a cricket match, entire country unites and then there is no one Hindu, Muslim, Sikh, or Christian, all are Indian! Similarly, no one is Punjabi, Tamilian, Telugu, Bengali, Marathi, Assamese, that time everyone is an Indian.

Similarly, there is no one from the upper caste, and lower caste at that time and all are Indian.

Other instances that unite us despite so many odds are cases of any disaster or attack on our mother nation.

Though we believe that these are the only times when we as a nation come together so let me remind you, there is one more instance, when we all stand united and abide it rigorously and that is any social malpractices where we all want to follow despite studying in best colleges, understanding the repercussions of it, going hand in hand with any western society but follow the roots for all those malpractices; we have reached Mars in search of life but have disregarded life on Earth by following those malpractices.

'Dowry' is one of the sins in our society that lies across length and breadth of our country. Here again, no one is spared irrespective of their colours, castes, creeds, and regions. This story is my effort to draw attention of the nation towards the sin and request everyone to rethink and start fighting against this evil. India has generated lots of respect across the World in last and now it is our duty to keep this malpractice away from our society and build a progressive country.

I hope you enjoy my effort that I have created with my words and take a pledge to fight against not only this evil but all others as well. Please do share your comments once you finish the story, your insight and feedback will go a long way in helping me improve my skills, passion and come out with better content in future.

Thank You.

Chapter - 1

[30 days ago]

It was six o'clock in the cool morning. Mr Roy Chaudhary had just reached his jogging track in the park.

Today he was late because his daughter, who normally jogged with him, was out of town. Her absence gave him an excuse to be lazy and sleep a few extra minutes. It was a perky, breezy Saturday morning. The park had a five-hundred meters track surrounded by many trees. The greenery made the park a soothing place for a morning jog. The musical chirping of the birds was a stress-buster. It was a haven far from the noisy vroommmm, vroommmm of the city's vehicles, insulated from the torture inflicted by youthful bikers zipping self-importantly along on bikes without silencers.

Mr Roy Chaudhary was a retired engineer. Post-retirement, he shifted to New Delhi where he owned a flat in Dwarka, a sub-city situated in the south-west of India's National Capital Region. Like any other sub-city or colonies, Dwarka had its own challenges- like scarcity of water and lack of good government hospitals. Apart from a few difficulties though, it remains one of the best-planned sub-cities and with all basic amenities. There are lush parks surrounded by apartments so the vehicle movement stays far from the parks and lets people enjoy their time in the lap of nature.

He put the water to boil for tea when he reached home. While the water was boiling, he fetched the newspapers. He looked around for something to clean his spectacles with and then cleaned them with a corner of the newspaper. The moment he added the tea leaves to the boiling water, the land-line phone rang with a harsh jangle. He lowered the heat on the stove and added the milk. He put the milk hurriedly in it and kept the gas flame on low and started walking to the drawing room to take the call.

"Who is calling so early in the morning?" he muttered to himself. "It can't be Putul. She wouldn't have time to call me at this hour!"

"Hello!" he said into the phone.

"Hello, may I talk to Ms Roy Chaudhary?" said a sweet voice.

"I'm afraid she is not at home right now. May I know who's calling?" he said.

"This is Swapna, a senior journalist from Times of India. Actually, her mobile seems to be switched off," said the voice.

"Maybe her phone battery has run out of juice," he said noncommittally. "She is out of town at present and will return by afternoon. Please call in the evening!"

"Sir, it is rather urgent! May I ask where she is right now?"

Though Mr Roy Chaudhary hesitated for a few seconds. But getting such calls for his daughter was not so new for him. Swapna was a well-known journalist whose articles he often read on TOI.

"She is in Mumbai. She is taking a Vistara Airline flight at 10:25 am so she will be home by afternoon," he said.

"Thanks, Sir! This is a great help. Have a good day, sir!" came the reply; the voice sounded palpably relieved.

"Good day to you too!" he replied.

He rushed to the kitchen and found his tea had boiled down to a mouthful of bitter and scalded liquid. He threw it away and began making tea again.

"The phone call ruined my tea! I will not read Swapna's column today as a mark of protest for keeping me away from my half cup of tea!"

He chuckled to himself, returned to the drawing room with his freshly brewed tea and started reading the newspaper.

* * *

After disconnecting her call with Mr Roy Choudhary, Swapna thought for a while, figuring out how to connect with Ms Roy Chaudhary. She did not want anyone else to cover the story which was yet to break. Once the news is out, it would be difficult for her to get any time from Ms Roy Chaudhary. A few seconds later, she called Ranjeet, her counterpart in Mumbai. Ranjeet wondered why Swapna was calling him so early in the morning.

"Hey, Swapna! How are you?" he said. "Is everything alright in Delhi or was there an earthquake during the night?" He chuckled.

"Shut up, Ranjeet! This is urgent and I need your help!" Swapna retorted.

Ranjeet sobered down and said, "Sorry Swapna, I didn't mean it. Tell me, how can I help you?"

"I know I can count on you anytime," she said, feeling relieved. "I just heard from my sources that Ms Roy Chaudhary is one of the nominees and a strong contender for the Ramon Magsaysay Award for her work. The final announcement will be made by the evening. I wanted to cover her story in advance but she is not in Delhi. She is taking a 10:25 am Vistara flight from Mumbai today," she said.

"Hmmm, interesting! So what do you need from me?" Ranjeet enquired.

"I want you to send a smart journalist on the same flight to interview her. In the next few minutes, I will send you a brief about her work and the questions I want her to be asked. Also, I will work out something so your junior gets a seat next to her. I will meet her and our journalist at Delhi airport and take it forward from there," Swapna finished hurriedly.

Ranjeet said, "Okay Swapna! You're asking for too much at short notice. Let me see what I can do!"

"Thanks, Ranjeet! It will be a great help if you can pull this off. I know, you can do it. This is just peanuts for you!" She giggled and disconnected the call.

She quickly collated some material and background story on Ms Roy Chaudhary on her laptop. She was surprised to see that nothing was available about her past except for the work she had done in the past ten years. She hurriedly drafted few questions and emailed it all to Ranjeet.

She called Ranjeet to check if he had received her mail.

"Yes, I got it. I had a word with Mrinalini and lined her up, briefing her in detail about the task. She will be leaving in some time for the airport. She will download all the questions on the way to the airport and will collect her ticket from the check-in desk at the airport." Ranjeet assured Swapna.

After the call, Swapna thought *How dumb I am! How am I to arrange a ticket for the journalist at the eleventh hour? This could be worked out somehow but would I be able to arrange for a seat next to Ms Roy Chaudhary so that our journalist could effectively utilise the time at hand?* She called her maid to bring her a cup of coffee to coax her exhausted grey cells in assisting her to assess the situation and come up with a solution.

After ten minutes, Swapna's maid brought the sugarless hot coffee; a new way to stay healthy.

After a couple of sips, she recalled that Gaurav, one of her team members, could help her out as he had recently covered a story about the rise of Vistara Airline in the Indian aviation space. Snapping her fingers victoriously, she called him immediately. Gaurav called her back in ten minutes and assured her that everything was arranged.

"But we might need to fly our journalist in business class," he said. Swapna agreed instantly.

* * *

When Mrinalini reached the airport, her phone flashed with a WhatsApp message. It was her ticket for the flight she was to board for Delhi. She went through the security check at the airport gate and picked up her boarding pass and proceeded towards boarding security check. Thereafter, she made herself comfortable on the corner seat at the airport lounge and downloaded the material which she might require during her journey. Though she had covered quite a few stories in past, she had never had a conversation with a philanthropist running an NGO.

Once she was done with her work, she went to one of the eating outlets and picked up a cup of green tea and some digestive cookies. She came back and sat down on her corner seat when her iPad beeped again; it was a mail from Ranjeet to help her to get the right material to cover this story. She knew that it was one of the high profile stories as no one really decided travels at such short notice-that too in business class.

She went through the background material she had been sent, including Ms Roy Choudhary's photo. She had never met the lady before. Mrinalini was a sports journalist, so she didn't know much about her.

* * *

Ms Roy Chaudhary reached the airport and asked for her boarding pass. The Vistara Airline representative informed her that her ticket had been upgraded; she being a Platinum category frequent flier customer. Although a little amazed as it doesn't usually happen, she took the upgrade in her stride and did not inquire any further. She moved to the lounge after collecting her upgraded boarding pass.

Ms Roy Chaudhary was in her late thirties. She was a tall, attractive and slim lady. Her dusky complexion showed her striking features to advantage. When she walked into a room, people naturally noticed her. Her impeccable grooming added greatly to her appeal.

She had donned a black blazer with a white shirt and black skinny tight trouser. She wore her hair loose and her sunglasses sat high on her head. A medium-sized golden colour duffle bag complemented her ensemble. Her high-heeled sandals rang a smart *tik-tok-tik.* People crossing her glanced at her appreciatively before moving on.

She did not find many people in the lounge. Heading straight to a food outlet to pick black coffee for herself, she hoped it would chase away her roaring headache. She had rushed to the airport in the morning as she was running late and felt exhausted now. Her black coffee would help her survive for the next few hours till she reached home.

After picking up her coffee mug, she looked around for a seat, when she saw Mrinalini sitting in a corner. When Mrinalini saw her, she smiled at her as she had recognised her. Ms Roy Chaudhary also reciprocated with a smile and sat two seats away from her and checked her mobile.

Mrinalini went back to reading the background info on Ms Roy Chaudhary. She knew she would get sufficient time to cover the story. Before she began the interview, she needed to be familiar with her past. She went through all the material that Ranjeet had shared quickly. She closed her iPad and walked over to a seat near Ms Roy Chaudhary.

Ms Roy Chaudhary glanced at her with a smile. Mrinalini reciprocated with an infectious grin.

"Hi! I am Mrinalini!" she said, holding out her hand.

"Hi! I am...." Before Ms Roy Chaudhary could complete her introduction, Mrinalini interrupted. "I know you, Ms Roy Chaudhary!"

Ms Roy Chaudhary was surprised, but smiled and said, "Thanks for recognising me."

"My pleasure, Ms Roy Chaudhary! Actually, I am a TOI journalist and want to cover your story. May we talk?" Ms Roy Chaudhary smiled and nodded.

Mrinalini picked up her iPad and opened the recording application and started recording the conversation. After making sure that the recording was working fine, she turned to her and started.

"Ms Roy Chaudhary, in the last ten years, your organization has enrolled 10000+ young enthusiasts. It has not only provided them with a base to make their career but has also settled them after marriage and each of them is happily married. How were you able to work that out?" Ms Roy Chaudhary smiled and answered.

"It is really encouraging to have around fifteen thousand families associated with our NGO. We have already settled eleven thousand needy people and now they are our evangelists and the supporting force behind our NGO. It is immensely satisfying to have achieved all I had envisioned ten years ago."

Mrinalini smiled.

"Was it difficult to convince people to join your organization?"

"I think, we have two kinds of people in our society-those who are open and willing to change and those who do not want to change. Because of all the emotional reasons mixed with their baseless arguments, the people of the latter category easily succeed in influencing them. We need someone to wake them up and once they are awake, they become catalysts for us."

Mrinalini smiled again and asked, "So even if you are targeting the first category of people, it is difficult to influence them, right?"

"It is. But you have to start from somewhere and I feel, I started with the right people. Instead of complaining about the hardships I faced, I did my work and continued to bring in a change, however small. I feel that even if you turn a few stones, you did work something out. I did my job without any expectation and hence I am happy with what I have managed to do."

Ms Roy Chaudhary smiled and Mrinalini reciprocated too.

"I tried to get some information about you from Google and other websites. However, I could not find any relevant information about you before your current journey, which started a decade ago." Mrinalini asked Ms Roy Chaudhary inquisitively.

Ms Roy Chaudhary smiled, "I am not a celebrity or from any family with a renowned background about which people are always eager to know. I am the part of 1.30 billion Indians who are regular, normal and hardworking people. So, I am sure that no one is keenly interested in investigating the story of an ordinary Indian and put it on the internet or some social media platform."

Mrinalini was surprised at Ms Roy Chaudhary's modest response. Keeping it for later though, she quickly changed the topic.

"You must surely have been inspired by something to start your NGO. Could you please share something about your motivation? Who inspired you or was there a sudden turn of events that you witnessed which gave you the idea of starting this NGO?"

"It is a very long story-my inspiration and the idea that started me on this journey. I don't think I can really do justice to it in the next fifteen minutes as I have to board a flight to Delhi."

"Don't worry. I am also boarding the same flight so we will get sufficient time to cover this," Mrinalini said reassuringly.

Ms Roy Chaudhary was surprised to hear this. But she kept mum and Mrinalini continued.

"Do tell me what inspired you to start this NGO. From where did you get the idea to support it financially and take the noble cause forward?"

Mrinalini's question took Ms Roy Chaudhary down memory lane. Her eyes bore a faraway look. It was evident that she was lost deep in her own thoughts. After a few minutes of silence, she took a deep breath and started her story.

"The story of a little girl inspired me. However, I am not sure, if you or your readers will be interested in that story as it is about a not so popular person. I would not like to share it," she said decisively.

"Our readers like all inspiring stories they can relate to. If this story inspired you, there will be many more people who may be inspired by your inspiration. Maybe people from the other category, as per your earlier comment, would move to the first category?" Mrinalini countered.

Ms Roy Chaudhary was convinced. She took a deep breath and began.

Chapter - 2

This is a story of a girl whose father, Om, was an engineer who worked with an ordinance factory. Ordinance Factories are the oldest industries in India's industrial space. The history of building ordinance factories in India dates back to the British era. Some of the factories are more than a century old now.

It was the autumn of 1979 when he was posted at the ordnance factory in the industrial area of Armapur, Kanpur, which was the industrial hub of the vast state of Uttar Pradesh. He was allotted a lavish bungalow as part of his perks. It had six large and spacious rooms with an approximate ceiling height of twenty to twenty-five feet at the centre. The sloped roof was covered using tiles in a distinct and attractive pattern. Since it was built during the British era and Kanpur witnesses harsh and chilling winters for a couple of months, each room had a fireplace. The chimney added to the aesthetics and the architecture of the bungalow.

There was a plush garden right in front of the magnificent bungalow. The garden was awash with green with over twenty fruit trees-mangoes, blackberry, jackfruit etc.- and a host of flowering bushes and plants adding to the loveliness of the garden. A servant's quarter was attached to the bungalow.

Om was a six-feet tall, dark and handsome guy. His uniform added to his smartness and enhanced his personality. A mechanical engineer, his Ambassador car was his passion. He devoted half of the month's first Sunday to the servicing and maintenance of his passion.

He was a jovial man who turned strict and sombre when it came to his family. Another striking character trait was his annoyance when he saw discrimination between girls and boys. A typical mannerism was for him to rub his head when he was anxious or stressed. One could easily see three lines on his forehead when he was in deep thought or nervous.

His thought process was clear and unambiguous. At work, he was strong and persuasive but could not change the mentality of his wife and mother who were biased towards boys.

There wasn't anything unusual in this since this mentality was pretty common in the society they lived in. He tried often to discuss and debate the issue with his wife and mother but there was no change in their stance.

His wife Jaya was a five-feet-four inch tall, lean and fair-complexioned lady. She was homely but she was also actively involved in the ordinance officer's ladies club. As the secretary, she was responsible for organizing many events.

One day, when Om came back from office in the evening, he found Jaya in the bedroom. It was unusual not to find her in the garden, waiting for him with the evening tea which they enjoyed having together. He found her lying down. She was feeling squeamish and giddy.

So Om called Ordinance Hospital and asked for doctor visit. Within the next fifteen minutes, a lady doctor arrived. Jaya was two months pregnant. The doctor mentioned that Jaya had some complications and would need complete bed rest for the next three months.

Om and Jaya were delighted with the happy news. That night, there was a small celebration at home.

Within the next couple of days, the news spread like wildfire. It was a small township and maids were the fastest carriers of news. People began dropping in with their best wishes.

Since there were complications and it was their first baby, both of them decided to call Om's mother to help and guide them. The care and supervision of the experienced elderly lady would help them a lot.

Om's mother arrived after a week. The first thing she did was to order a big portrait of Om to be hung opposite the couple's bed so Jaya would see it continuously and would be blessed with a baby boy just like Om.

Om was not convinced but the resolute ladies forced him to comply with their demands. In a couple of days, the wall in front of their bed had a large black and white collage of Om's and Jaya's pictures. This was Om's idea to have pictures of both of them, instead of having just his.

His mother and wife were not happy. However, they did not want to argue with him so said nothing.

* * *

Winter had just arrived. Jaya's complications were aggravated though doctors didn't find any reason to it. She was on complete bed rest but that didn't seem to improve her health.

She knew it was a matter of a few months but it wasn't easy for her. Her nausea was constant. Even the smell of the food made her throw up. She lost weight and became weaker. This added to her complications. After the fifth month, the doctor declared that Jaya was probably having twins, which added to the excitement of the family.

Jaya spent the whole day in her room reading religious books and looking at the collage on the wall in front of her bed.

* * *

It is rightly said that time, whether good or bad, passes on. Winter was about to end and make way for spring. Fresh, green leaves were replacing the dry brown winter foliage. The entire garden was covered with dry leaves. Days had turned warmer and balmy. The enchanting greenery made the place scenic and mesmerising.

Spending time outdoors, sitting or walking, were immensely enjoyable. Jaya had stabilized. She was encouraged to go for a walk in the mornings and evenings. Since they had a huge garden, she took her walks there. It was during her very first morning walks that she realised the beauty in her garden. There were many flowers blossoming.

She enjoyed this time by concentrating on nature's gifts like the chirping of birds, fall of leaves, various colourful butterflies in the garden etc.

At last, the much awaited day finally came. Jaya was in labour. She had been admitted to the hospital. Om and his mother were anxiously waiting at the reception.

The doctor came out of the labour room and asked Om to come to her cabin. She knew the family pretty well so it was a difficult conversation for her too. She removed her spectacles and put them on the table.

She rubbed her hands together nervously and said, "Om, with profound sadness I must inform you that Jaya has complications in her delivery and we need to do a caesarean-section for her. I am not able to get the heartbeat of both the kids so I need to operate without wasting any more time. But I want to know your decision before moving ahead."

"Doctor, p-p-please do whatever best you can do for Jaya!" Om stammered.

The doctor immediately rushed in to complete the formalities for the surgery and begin the caesarean procedure.

The next few hours were stressful for Om. He paced restlessly from one corner of the hospital to the next. He was drowning in a sea of anxiety and suspense. His body language betrayed his worry.

After four hours, the doctor came out and declared, "We could save only one child. The second child had died in the womb itself. Thankfully we operated on time else it would have been dangerous for the second child and to Jaya." There was another grim blow waiting for him. "Jaya should not conceive now. If she does, it would be a matter of life and death for her!"

Om was happy Jaya and the baby were safe. He did not want to lose Jaya, his soul-mate, at the cost of another child. He was happy yet sad as he was celebrating the birth of the one child and mourning the demise of another.

After being kept under strict observation for the next four-five hours, Jaya was shifted to a private ward from the operation theatre. When Om met her, she was very sad as she had lost one child. Om tried to console her but she cried continuously. Om tried his best to calm her down, knowing this wailing and mourning would definitely have an adverse effect on her health.

Finally, the nurse arrived with their baby in her hands-a tiny blessing wrapped up in white linen. It was a girl. Her eyes were closed and her lips and cheeks were pink. Sticky hair covered half of her forehead. The nurse came to Om and handed the baby to him. Om tried to hold her gently but he was awkward with her. Afraid he might hurt the baby, he glanced at Jaya intending for her to take the baby from his arms. But she kept her eyes closed and shifted to the other side, refusing to glance at her newborn.

For the next one hour, Om walked about the room with his little angel in his arms. That hour was the beginning of an everlasting bond between the father and daughter.

After a couple of days, Jaya and her daughter were discharged from the hospital and came back home. Om was very happy about getting a daughter as cute as a doll. But things were different for Jaya and Om's mother. They were not happy. They wanted a boy. But they never shared their feelings with Om. Om was so busy with his work and playing with his doll in the evening, that he never noticed anything unusual at home.

Since he didn't notice, he never realised that Jaya was unhappy. She wanted a son but she could not share her feelings with Om as she knew her husband did not believe in discriminating between a boy and a girl. Any discussion with him on this topic would never yield any result and would take unnecessary strain at home.

After a few months, the naming ceremony of the little girl was organised. The entire house was decorated with lamps and each tree in the garden was lit up with thousands of colourful lights. Every nook and corner of the house was illuminated, eliminating even a trace of darkness. The decoration and arrangements were such that even the decoration done for the festival of lights *Diwali* looked diminutive. Hundreds of invites were sent out for the occasion.

On the day of the ceremony, Om was busy with the arrangements, trying to make sure everything was as perfect as his princess deserved. He wanted everyone to remember the day for years to come. In the morning after the *Pooja* ceremony, the priest selected the doll's name as *Pavani*, another name of *Goddess Ganga*.

In the evening, the little girl wore a white fairy dress. Her grandmother put a black mark from *kajal* on her chin to protect her from the evil's eye. That was the happiest day in Om's life. Many people asked him why he had organized a lavish function for a girl-child.

"If you spend all the money on her naming ceremony, then what will you do for her marriage?" they asked.

Many such questions were thrown at Om but he went on unperturbed with just one answer, "Time will give you the best answer. It would be one of the most lavish functions and the privileged ones who will attend it will see for themselves!"

Suddenly there was an announcement which brought both Ms Roy Chaudhary and Mrinalini back to the present.

"May I have your attention, please? The Vistara flight to Delhi UK-994 has been delayed by an hour. The inconvenience caused is deeply regretted."

Both took a deep breath and looked at each other. After taking a pause for few seconds, Ms Roy Chaudhary asked Mrinalini, "Am I revealing too many personal and in-depth details? I think I should not share this story in such detailed form."

"No, no! This is fine, Ms Roy Chaudhary!" Mrinalini countered.

"But I think, I am going too much in detail and I am not sure if I should. Will the readers be interested in such a detailed story or will you find a relevant portion out of it?" Ms Roy Chaudhary enquired, hesitating.

"I don't think there is any problem as you can share the whole story and we will pick and choose the relevant portions out of it." Mrinalini tried to convince her.

Does it make sense to share someone's story in such detail?" Ms Roy Chaudhary stressed her point yet again.

"You are not sharing someone's story. You are sharing your inspiration so I don't think you should hesitate."

Though Ms Roy Chaudhary seemed to be convinced by Mrinalini's point of view, her body language didn't show the conviction. Ms Roy Chaudhary was still lost in deep thought, her gaze fixed at one point. The movement of her index fingers signalled that she was still in doubt about her decision. Mrinalini sensed her mental conflict and diverted the conversation, "Do you know Swapna Ma'am? She wants your story in tomorrow's TOI edition. You know, she normally does not pick any story unless she is convinced that this story has substance and she surely believes that your story has great substance." Mrinalini grinned.

Ms Roy Chaudhary smiled at Mrinalini. On hearing Swapna's name, she did not argue. She knew Swapna and had met with her on a few previous occasions. She knew Swapna was a well-respected name in the journalist fraternity. She stood up and asked, "Let me get some coffee. Do you also want it?"

Mrinalini nodded and they both walked over to the breakfast corner to pick up the coffee from the coffee machine.

On returning, Mrinalini asked, "Shall we continue?"

Ms Roy Chaudhary smiled and continued...

* * *

Chapter - 3

Pavani was her father's princess, she realised that early in her age based on her interaction with both her father and mother. She used to wait for her father to come back from office. She always got everything that she wanted without having to ask for it.

Pavani knew that she was her father's pampered girl and she felt proud whenever someone called out *here comes daddy's girl!*

* * *

Monsoon had arrived. There were heavy showers in July. The city soon wore a lush green look. Not just the trees, but the entire place became green. There was a fresh aroma in the air. Leaves looked greener after the summer dust had been washed away. The moist soil was resplendent with petrichor. Birds had built their nest in the trees. The garden was lively with the chirping of sparrows and cuckooing of koels. Fragrance and music filled the air. Peacocks danced majestically in the rain.

Pavani was around seven years at that time. She enjoyed the rain and loved riding her bicycle in the garden. Whenever it rained, she waited indoors for it to stop. As soon as it did, she was out with her bicycle. Her clothes became dirty and wet because she had tried racing with the butterflies. Her mother had warned her many times, but like other children of her age, she was experiencing the rain like never before. She continued enjoying the rain in her own way.

When there was twilight and darkness started engulfing the entire area, her mother took her inside and made her take a bath changed her clothes. Pavani shivered as she was exposed to rain for around four hours. Her mother scolded her for her carelessness and just like any other child, she ignored her scolding. She was covered with linen so that she could feel its warmth.

Soon the house was full of noisy crickets, one of the most common insects found during rainy season. One of the mesh doors was left ajar and thousands of crickets entered the house.

All the insects were making a buzzing sound, which was very annoying. Pavani was scared by the sound and started crying. Her mother tried to console her but nothing could pacify her. She wasn't ready to listen to her soothing words. She wanted to be consoled by her father who was not in town. Jaya tried to get her to eat her dinner but she ate very little.

Jaya asked Pavani to go to her room and said that she would join in some time. The little girl could not gather the courage to go into her room alone. She was still terrified by the buzzing sound and those flying crickets, even though her mother told her that there was nothing to be scared about.

After an hour, Jaya finished her work and took Pavani to her room. For the next one hour, she tried to put Pavani to sleep but the girl was too scared. Her mother sang a lullaby and soothed her but Pavani continuously looked at the ceiling where those monsters that were in thousands in number, were flying just above her.

When Jaya found that it was difficult to get Pavani to fall asleep in her room, she brought Pavani to her own room. When Pavani was reassured that she would not be alone, she slept. Subsequently, Jaya too fell asleep.

During the night, when Jaya got up to use the restroom, she found that Pavani was shivering. When she touched her, she found her body was burning with fever. Jaya was shocked. She fetched the thermometer to check Pavani's temperature.

The temperature was almost 101°F. She immediately gave Pavani a spoonful of Paracetamol and waited for the fever to subside.

That night was scary and long for both Jaya and Pavani. Pavani was frightened from insects and Jaya was frightened with her health

Finally, it was dawn. And the long, scary night was over. Jaya took Pavani to the doctor in the morning and gave her the medicines prescribed by him.

After coming home, Pavani lay on her bed and looked out through the small window. It was still drizzling. She wanted to go out but didn't have the courage to ask her mother if she could go. She contented herself by looking out of the window and admired the drenched garden.

After some time, she asked her mother, "Mom, when will Papa come back?"

"Why are you asking baby?" Jaya asked her.

"I hope he will be back before evening!"

Jaya gave her a surprised look. *Why is she so desperate to have her father back before evening?* Jaya thought.

Pavani continued, "Mom, I want to talk to Papa about something important."

"Yes, my dear baby. He will be back by evening. You can talk to him then."

Pavani took a deep breath and heaved a sigh of relief.

After this short conversation with her mother, Pavani's day was spent waiting for her father. In the evening, when Om returned, Pavani was the first one to meet him and climb into his arms. He put his bag down and picked her up immediately and gave her a gentle hug and kissed her cheeks and forehead. Pavani was now at peace. She knew that her father would have a solution to all her problems. When Om found out that Pavani was running a temperature, he asked her what the reason was.

"What happened to my little princess?"

"I am frightened, Papa!" she whispered.

"Of whom?" Om asked.

"Papa, there were so many monsters flying above me and making a buzzing sound. I was terrified as they were just above my bed," she said, breathing hard.

"But you are my brave princess!" Om comforted her and tried to reassure her.

"Yes, but they were so many."

"Okay, so you should have told mom about it."

"Mom wouldn't have listened to me and would have also scolded me so I didn't tell her anything," she whispered.

"No problem, my dear princess! We will chase away all the monsters before we go to sleep. That's my promise to you!" said Om lovingly.

Pavani nodded, reassured and gave a high-five to her father. As darkness began to set in, Om was surprised to see many crickets inside the house. At first, he thought of creating smoke inside the house but it was too late and they would have had to go out of the house until the smoke cleared. He'd have to come up with another option, he thought.

Pavani was confident that her father would definitely do something about those monsters so she could sleep peacefully that night.

When Om saw her, she was frightened and he understood that her health was not good due to her fear of crickets. After much thought, he planned to kill all the insects. He closed all the doors and rolled couple of newspapers to make a small soft stick and started hitting all the insects. For the next couple of hours, he made sure that there was no cricket inside the house. With each insect was being killed, Pavani gained more strength and was hopeful that soon there will be no insects in the house. After a few minutes, she clapped on each hit and helped her father to hunt down the insects in the entire house.

Pavani felt secure and was immensely relieved. She gave a big hug to her father.

Pavani's connection with her father was obvious. She believed in him totally and felt completely secure with him. Their bonding delighted Jaya. She couldn't help but smile and feel elated.

Pavani was hale and hearty the next morning. She was back to being a spinning top in the house and enjoyed the rainy weather just like she did the day before.

When Ms Roy Chaudhary took a pause, Mrinalini asked with a child-like enthusiasm, "Wow!!! Was it the only incident or were there many?"

Ms Roy Chaudhary smiled and replied, "There were so many, but I recalled this one as I liked her affection and the quick action by her father to any of her demands. He never thought twice to fulfil any wish his princess had."

"Interesting! What happened next?"

Ms Roy Chaudhary continued...

* * *

Chapter - 4

The life is movement. A child's life is particularly so.

Pavani spent her childhood like other kids. Her father fulfilled all her wishes. He did not stop to think twice before rushing to fulfil her demands, though Jaya didn't like it many times. But neither Om nor Pavani paid heed to her disapproval.

Pavani made no demands of her mother, never sure if they would be met. She kept all her pleas to herself until she got a chance to share them with her father. For him, there was only one thumb rule-to fulfil all her requests as soon as they were made. The father-daughter bond grew stronger with each day.

Om was transferred to Jabalpur and Pavani completed her education there. Her schooling was over and she was to go to college. Om too had been transferred to Ambernath, another unit of ordinance factory in Maharashtra, he decided to quit and take voluntary retirement. He was looking for a place where he could settle post-retirement and Pavani could complete her further studies. Finally, Om and Jaya zeroed in to settle in Kanpur.

Jaya also accepted his decision as the major focus was now on Pavani's higher education which was about to start in a few months' time. With the idea accepted at home, Om decided to discuss it with his boss.

On the very next day, Om discussed it with his boss, the General Manager of the company. A thorough gentleman, he understood Om's problem and supported his transfer to Kanpur so that he could relocate to the city without having to retire from his job.

Once everything was settled, Om purchased a house in Kanpur's Yashoda Nagar locality that was on the outskirts of the city but was developing rapidly.

When he was transferred to Kanpur, instead of shifting to ordinance accommodation, he shifted his family to the house he bought. Though it was not sprawling bungalow as he would have been allotted officially, it was a large three bedroom house, sufficient enough for the Om's small family of three. Although Pavani missed her group at the ordinance house society, it was an exciting experience to be living in your own house.

Pavani was around eighteen-years-old at that time and had cleared her twelfth grade. She was ready to join college and was looking forward to it. From ordinance's township, the college was at quite a distance so it was a good decision for them to live in their own house which was closer to college.

After a couple of weeks, she took admission in BA Economics at the famous The Christ Church College, one of the oldest colleges in Kanpur. She aimed at becoming a microeconomist. This college was built during the British era. Being one of the most popular and reputed colleges, it attracted many students from far and wide.

She was nervous on her first day of college. It was exciting to meet other enthusiastic students just like her who had dreams of many achievements in their eyes. The college would be the launching pad for their future to take off.

In the class on the first day, teachers and students introduced themselves. Pavani met a girl called Vaishali who lived at Kidwai Nagar. After attending the introductory lectures with her, Pavani began to feel hungry. She couldn't focus. Unable to bear her hunger, Pavani asked her, "Vaishali, I am feeling hungry. What about you?"

Vaishali also nodded.

"Oh great! Let's find the canteen and eat something then!" said Pavani happily.

The canteen was not large. It was an open outlet on the college premises. It was a hub for lovebirds, future planners, a place for forging or breaking friendships and a resting place for souls exhausted by academics. One could find all kinds of street food items like *Samosa, Kachori,* Sandwich, tea, coffee etc. over here. Not only were the items moderately priced but also the people serving the food made it a point that the students were comfortable. They made the canteen a popular hangout on the college premises.

When Pavani and Vaishali reached the canteen, they found it full of noisy students. Some were meeting each other for the first time. Others were old friends and were meeting each other after a semester break.

Pavani and Vaishali had never had such an experience before so it looked exciting. There were many reunions in the canteen as it was the first day after the college break. Students were greeting each other, sharing what they did during the break, ordering food and gobbling it up as soon as it arrived. The commotion was new and fascinating to both, the first-time college girls.

Pavani and Vaishali mutually agreed to have a *bread pakora* each. At the counter, Pavani paid for two *bread pakoras.* Before she could pick the plates and carry them to Vaishali, a smart lad picked up one *bread pakora* and ate it. Though Pavani was a simple, quiet and sensible girl, her hunger had turned her irritable. She was fuming and yelled at the boy, "Hey that's mine! How dare you eat my *pakora* without even asking?"

"So, what? I haven't committed a crime!" the boy reverted, taken aback by her outrage.

"We paid for those *pakoras* and told the boy at the counter to put it on the plates for us!" Pavani raised her voice.

"Oh, is that the issue? Don't worry, I will pay for it!" He replied casually.

To Pavani, it looked like arrogance. She was even more annoyed. It seemed that far from being sorry, he couldn't imagine what the hubblaboo was all about. This made her angrier still. She snatched the half-eaten piece of *pakora* from his hand and threw it in the dustbin. The boy was too taken aback by her quick reflexes to react. Pavani had been super quick. When he looked around, he saw everyone staring at him. He just apologised and moved out of the canteen with his friend, without waiting for her response.

Vaishali picked up the remaining one and divided it into half. Both of them shared it and ate quietly.

The next day, when Pavani entered the classroom, Vaishali was already sitting there. When Vaishali saw her, she greeted her with a smile and pointed her to sit next to her.

"Hi, Vaishali!" Pavani said with excitement.

"Hi, Pavani!" Vaishali replied with the same enthusiasm.

Pavani saw someone's notebook on the seat next to Vaishali. "Whose books are these?" she asked.

"No idea. I think you can shift it to another desk and sit down," Vaishali suggested.

Pavani did as Vaishali suggested and sat down next to her.

Just then, the boy with whom Pavani had a tussle in the canteen entered the class with his friend. He went to Pavani's seat, picked up her notebooks and threw them out of the classroom. It was over in seconds. Pavani could not comprehend what happened and stared blankly at the boy. She could neither move from her place nor react.

Before this moment, there was a lot of noise and hustle-bustle in the classroom. But after this incident, there was pin drop silence.

"How dare you shift my notebooks without asking me?" he yelled furiously.

Pavani was too shocked to say anything to him. Vaishali intervened and raised her voice.

"Why are you so arrogant? Yesterday, you fought with us at the canteen and now you being rude again!"

"I did not start it yesterday, it was you! And today again. Why did you shift my notebook? If both of you want to sit together, either you should have come early or should have shifted to the back bench."

"We just shifted your notebook one desk away. You are still sitting in the same row! Is it really a big deal that you have taken such an extreme step to throw her notebooks outside the class? Don't you know that books and notebooks are to be respected? Goddess *Saraswati* resides in them and you have thrown them away so disrespectfully! Don't you have any manners?"

It looked like he had no answer to Vaishali's bang-on-target argument. By then, the entire class had also started whispering. Since it was just the second day of the college and everyone was looking for friends, he didn't want to look bad and continue the fight. Another boy, who was standing next to him, went to the classroom door, grabbed the books and gave it to Pavani.

Just then the professor came in and both the boys immediately moved to their seats next to Pavani before the lecture began.

Noticing her far-away look, Vaishali pinched and whispered to Pavani to pay attention. That's when Pavani realised that the class had started.

After the class, both the boys came over. The boy who had thrown Pavani's books out said, "I am sorry! Trust me, I am not like this. But yesterday's incident really got to me and I behaved egotistically with you. I hope you can understand and forgive everything that has happened in the past two days."

Pavani was speechless. She hadn't expected an apology. She looked at him without saying a word. The lad extended his hand to Pavani and said, "Friends?"

Pavani was still uncertain. Before she could say anything, Vaishali stood up, shook hands with him and made Pavani shake hands too.

"Friends!" She chuckled with excitement.

"I am Raj... Raj Awasthi..." The boy introduced himself.

"I am Vaishali and she is Pavani."

"Why are you speaking? Is she dumb?"

Pavani glared at him. Then she grinned and they all laughed.

"Hi! I am Amit Kumar. Raj and I became friends yesterday. Now, we are a group of four. That's cool. Isn't it?" the other boy introduced himself.

It was the beginning of a new friendship.

* * *

Chapter - 5

The next one year was full of challenges interspersed with lots of enjoyment-so different from the disciplined life of school. The altered life had new learnings, new friends, new plans, new dreams, new aspirations and more freedom than ever. Life took its own course and kept everyone busy in their own world. Many had plans of becoming scientists, investment bankers, IT professionals, professors or bureaucrats.

Plans were short-lived. Some died their own death while others were made on Monday and as the week ended, were murdered after a seemingly serious debate on its pros and cons. There were many wishes and unfulfilled dreams that shaped up. There were mental conflicts and thoughts zipped past at a lightning speed, refusing to zero down to a single wish or plan.

The metamorphosis taking place within her classmates did not leave Pavani untouched. She too was transformed from a meek and quiet girl to an outgoing extrovert. She was no longer the girl in a neatly ironed uniform with oiled hair tightly braided. She was now a five-foot-four-inches tall damsel with a dusky, glowing complexion. Pavani had sharp features and curly hair which added a sparkle to her beauty. Her sense of dressing style saw a major shift. She now wore western dresses instead of the traditional ones that she once wore. Though her mother didn't like it but was unable to express her disapproval as Pavani had the full support of her father. She was getting smarter with each passing day. In spite of all these exterior changes, she was still a very soft spoken girl, focused on her studies. She aimed at getting an MBA degree after completing her graduation.

Apart from the change in her lifestyle and aspirations, one thing that never changed was her favourite Bollywood actress. She was still a diehard fan of Kajol. She had watched almost all her movies, more than once. If there was a discussion about Kajol and someone made an uncomplimentary comment about her, they had to bear the brunt of Pavani's anger. Her entire gang was aware of it, so whenever someone wanted to drag a discussion longer or wanted to pull her in it, they typically picked up the topic involving Kajol and said something negative about the actress. This would stretch the discussion longer than expected or as desired by the person who initiated it.

Though Pavani was a confident girl, one could easily make out when she was nervous or tense. A typical mannerism was to rub her fingers with her thumb. This was a sign of anxiety in her.

Vaishali was five-feet-two-inches tall. She had a fair complexion with sharp features. She was an easy going girl. She wanted to enjoy her life and was of a friendly nature. She loved to help everyone, whether she liked that person or not. Her life's mantra was simple- *help the needy and enjoy life as if there is no tomorrow*.

Raj was six-feet tall. He was a smart guy and was focused on his studies and building a glittering career. Just like Pavani, he too wanted to go for a Masters in management after completing his graduation. Raj was a very soft-spoken and good-at-heart person. He always obeyed his parents and never went against them in life. Though he never had any arguments with anyone, Pavani was somehow an exception. On several other occasions after their first encounter, they had many points of disagreement that led to fights and arguments. Most of the time, Vaishali was the bridge to bring these two seemingly poles-apart people together again after a heated discussion.

Amit was the fourth person in this gang. He was an average looking person with a height of around five-feet-seven inches. Though he did not have an impressive personality, he always made some highly impressive statements that were hard to believe. These doubtful statements of his earned him the name *Fenku* or the *Fabulist.* Slowly, this became his nickname and he became famous in entire college for his tall tales. He did not like his nickname but couldn't say anything to anyone. Whenever he raised this issue with his friends, they told him to be mindful of the things he said. They told him to talk sense and choose sensible statements while conversing.

Pavani, Vaishali, Raj and Amit discussed many topics of different natures and from a variety of fields. As a result of a discussion amongst four people of a distinct nature, there were disagreements, dislikes, fights and heated discussions. The conversation also had some positive highlights like sharing aspirations, concurrences on topics of similar interests and talking about likes etc. There was just one exception to this rule. There was no discord whenever the two girls-Pavani and Vaishali-shared their dreams with each other. They had a heart-to-heart talk and giggled and enjoyed their conversation with ease.

Soon it was the end of February. Exam dates were about to be declared. Winter had just passed and spring was about to arrive. Old leaves were falling, giving way to the fresh leaves. Due to the changing weather and scenery, a morning walk seemed so soothing and energizing. One could easily see an increase in the number of people going out for a morning walk, to enjoy the scenery, whilst taking care of their health.

One nice breezy morning, as the morning-walk crowds were returning home, Pavani was ready to go to college. She was dressed in a beautiful pink top and slim-fit blue jeans. She had a small bag in her hands. She headed to Vaishali's house as they both planned to go together to college to check the exam dates to be announced that day.

When she reached Vaishali's house and knocked on the door, Vaishali's mother answered the door. When Pavani asked for Vaishali she said Vaishali was still asleep. Pavani was surprised as they had together planned to go to the college.

Vaishali was fast asleep in her room. Her room was totally unorganized; a couple of books were lying next to her pillow. The study table had loads of books and notebooks. Right next to the study table, there was a dressing table and almost all the items were lying haphazardly on it. Pavani took a deep breath and picked up the books and notebooks and quickly arranged everything on the study table. She then sat next to her pillow.

Looking down affectionately at Vaishali, Pavani wondered how one could sleep so soundly when exams are just around the corner. *Is Vaishali not at all worried about the exams? She is such a careless girl. What will happen to her? How she will manage her life?* On an impulse, she picked up a cotton ball from the dressing table and rolled it up to make a thin thread. Slowly, she inserted the tip into Vaishali's ear.

When it touched her ear, Vaishali immediately reacted and tried to remove what was going inside her ear. Pavani was very quick to remove it. Vaishali turned to the other side. Though Pavani was not mischievous normally, she could not miss this opportunity.

Vaishali also joined in with others and criticized Kajol, how could she forgive her? This was her revenge. She was enjoying it. She grinned as she put the cotton thread in Vaishali's other ear. When the thread touched her ear, Vaishali changed sides again. Pavani tried it again but this time, she was not quick enough to pull it out in time and Vaishali caught the thread. She first thought it must be her brother who was trying to wake her up. She growled menacingly without opening her eyes. "Baua, do not do it. I will tell mom!"

Pavani giggled and Vaishali opened her eyes. When she found Pavani sitting next to her, she shot up immediately, brushing the hair off her face. Her eyes were still heavy with sleep. She yawned and asked, "Was it you who was disturbing my sleep? I was in the midst of a beautiful dream!"

"Hey, we need to go to college! We discussed yesterday over the call that we will go to college in the morning. Why are you still not ready?" Pavani said loudly.

"There's no need to go college. Raj came last night and shared the exam schedule. I thought of calling but it was already 9 o'clock. So I thought I'll give you a call early in the morning but I could not get up early. Sorry for that."

"Raj? Did he come here? He could have come to my house as well and shared the exam schedule!" Pavani exclaimed peevishly.

"Are you jealous?" Vaishali asked with a naughty wink.

Pavani was not ready for that question. She fumbled.

"Wh-wh-why should I be jealous? A-a-are you in your senses?"

"He shared the schedule with me but not with you, so I thought you were jealous!" Vaishali chuckled.

"It is okay. He lives closer to your house so he shared it with you and anyway you must have told him you'll share it with me."

Before Vaishali could respond, her mother entered with two cups of tea and some biscuits.

Both the girls smiled. Vaishali's mother smiled back at them and turned to Pavani.

"Do you also sleep until noon?"

"Mom!!!" exclaimed Vaishali retorted before Pavani could reply.

"Exams are about to start in two weeks. It is time to study and you are wasting your time sleeping! I am not asking you to help me out with any household chores. At least, you should utilise your time for something fruitful." Vaishali's mother chided, annoyed at her sleeping till late and her casual attitude.

Vaishali was about to crack a joke and lighten the atmosphere but saw that her mother was in a *no-nonsense* mood so quickly resumed a sombre look.

"I will definitely start serious studies from today. Yesterday Raj left a bit late and after that, I was any way studying late so couldn't get up early in the morning."

"Morning is the best time to study as our concentration is at its peak then." Her mother countered and left the room. Though her mother went out of the room, Vaishali was still staring at the door and there was complete silence in the room when Pavani spoke.

"Your mom is right. We should now start focusing on our studies as there is hardly any time left for the exams."

Vaishali turned towards Pavani and retorted, "Don't behave like my mom. You still have some time to play that role."

Before Pavani could say anything, she started laughing. Both of them then had tea.

"Pavani, may I ask you a question?" said Vaishali.

"Yes, why not? And since when do you need permission?"

"Hope you will answer me honestly. You will not hide anything."

Pavani nodded.

"Pavani, we have both known Raj for almost a year now. What do you think of him?"

Pavani thought, *what a silly question is this? What do you think means what? What is going in Vaishali's mind? What does she want to know?*

When Vaishali saw that Pavani pondered over the question and did not reply quickly, she chuckled.

"So, I was right," she said.

Pavani knew it was time to clear the air. She said, "What do you mean by think? He is like a friend."

"Are you sure?"

Another shot from point-blank range by Vaishali. *Is she really in her senses*, Pavani thought?

"Yes, I am sure. Why are you asking such a silly question?"

"I am asking this question because I sensed something during our treat last week," said Vaishali.

"Really? What did you sense, may I ask?" Pavani asked.

"You remember we were planning to organise Baua's birthday party last week? I was telling you not to do it. But you were very excited and ready to organise the entire party."

"Yeah, so what does this prove?"

"Let me finish. Why are you in such a hurry to jump down my throat?" Vaishali said holding up a hand.

"We discussed and planned the party at home. You convinced my mom to help us organize it. When you started preparing for it, no one came forward to help you except Raj."

Pavani was wondering where it was leading to. *So what if only Raj helped? What on earth is she implying?*

Vaishali fell silent and tried to gauge Pavani's thoughts.

"I don't know what is going on in your mind! What story are you cooking? Raj is our oldest friend. We connected with him on day one. What's the big deal if Raj helped out?" Pavani asked, perplexed.

"I agree he is one of our oldest acquaintances in the college. But we're a group of eight to ten friends. Friends and friendships aren't measured by the number of days they are known; instead, it is the bond that matters. Why didn't any other friend in the group come forward to help you to organise the party? Why could only Raj sense that you needed help in getting everything in place?"

Pavani was still not sure what Vaishali was getting at. *Why is she going on and on about Raj?* She was getting irritated with such silly questions, so instead of dragging it, she told Vaishali to come straight to the point.

Vaishali smirked, "So my suspicion was right."

"Why are you making such a mystery of it? Why can't you straightaway come to the point?"

"Ok-k-k-ay, don't get hyper! I will tell you straight out.

"When Raj agreed to help you to organize that party, I was not aware of his intentions. While organizing that party, I noticed that he was trying to be with you most of the time, at any moment he could. When you were decorating the place, a small task you could do on your own, he was there to help you out. When everyone was dancing at the party, he was the one who was shying away. But when you joined, he also chimed in. I think he is in love."

"What! Are you crazy?!" Pavani was taken aback. This is the last thing she expected. Vaishali didn't say anything, letting her observation sink in.

"I'm sure you are mistaken. There is no such thing in his or in my heart. You're turning into a story-teller. Why don't you choose this as your profession?" Pavani declared, nettled.

"If you want to accept it, fine! If not, then leave it. I am not going to fight about it," countered Vaishali.

"I don't want to think of anything except my exams right now. The dates are already declared. From here on, I will concentrate on my exams and study alone, though earlier I planned to do it together."

Vaishali was taken aback and didn't say a word. She stood up and copied the exam schedule on a sheet of paper and handed it to Pavani. Her hurt showed plainly on her face. Pavani put the schedule in her bag and left.

Ms Roy Chaudhary took a pause, she could see the sparkle in Mrinalini's eyes. "Looks like you are enjoying every bit of this story," she observed.

"Why did Pavani react in such a way? It was a common discussion between friends." Mrinalini questioned Ms Roy Chaudhary.

Ms Roy Chaudhary smiled. "I think, until then Pavani had never thought of anything except her studies or her family. She knew that her father had many dreams for her career and marriage. She couldn't imagine doing anything to hurt her father."

"Hmmm. So what happened next?"

Before Ms Roy Chaudhary could continue, there was an announcement.

"Passengers of Vistara Airline flight number UK-994 Mumbai to Delhi are requested to proceed to Gate Number 8 to board the flight."

Both of them smiled and picked up their bags and started walking towards the gate.

After getting into the aircraft, both of them settled down in their seats. Mrinalini asked Ms Roy Chaudhary if she could continue with her story.

Ms Roy Chaudhary smiled and continued...

Chapter - 6

For the next two-three months, everyone's routine revolved around studies. All discussions were limited to their studies, syllabus of the exams, important questions, how to mug up answers-and how to stay awake and alert during the night.

The college reopened in July after a semester break. The students were rejuvenated and excited to start a fresh session. They now had a new syllabus, books and teachers. The groups met as usual and shared their experiences of the break. Amit Kumar had something special to share from his experience. During the recess, the group was in the canteen when Amit opened up.

"I had a great time during the summer break."

Everyone looked at him in amazement and listened with great interest as he had already announced that he had something unusual to share with them. Raj sat next to him and was least bothered in his revelations as he knew that anything that Amit said would be hard to believe.

"During the summer break, I went to Hyderabad and had a great time there."

Everyone became interested in knowing more about it. He continued with increased enthusiasm when he saw how curious everyone was.

"But I do not want to share as you guys will also try my trick here."

Everybody laughed as they all knew that he would first create the curiosity and then would share something which would be good to dig in for the next few days.

Everyone waited for him to speak but when he didn't, Raj asked, "Why don't you share, Amit? We all are excited."

When he heard Raj spoke, he knew the stage was set for him, so he started.

"I went to my uncle's house in Nagpur. When my uncle saw that I was getting bored, he suggested that I go to Hyderabad for a couple of days during the weekend and enjoy my time over there. I liked his idea. Vinod, my cousin, and I went to Hyderabad by bus. It was a night service bus that started from Nagpur in the evening and reached Hyderabad in the morning."

Amit took a deep breath and continued, "Both of us boarded the bus and found that our seats were in the middle of the bus. Two girls were sitting in the next row. They were really pretty and stylish. We both were very excited to have set on a journey that might be an adventure worth remembering. Vinod and I share a good rapport; we are more friends than cousins.

"We wanted to make an impression on the girls. We started talking to each other hoping we were coming across as intelligent, knowledgeable and sensitive. We made sure we were loud enough so that they could hear us."

Everyone in the group listened to this narrative wondering what the big revelation was about. Amit paused to look around and was gratified to find that he had the attention of his audience.

"Around 10 pm the bus stopped at a *dhaba* for dinner and one of the girls got down. The other one tried to get something from her bag kept on the luggage rack just above our seats.

"Since the passage was narrow, we waited for her to finish as there was hardly any space for anyone to cross. Suddenly, she cried out in pain. We looked at her and saw that she was holding her left thumb with her right hand and was obviously in pain. Her left thumb was bleeding. The thumb-nail had got caught between the bag and the rack and had torn off, taking some skin with it. I pulled the bag down immediately and put it down on her seat. She opened the zip and took out her hair band and wallet from the bag. Before she could say thanks, both of us got down from the bus."

Raj could hardly believe Amit's story and made a face. Pavani, who sat right in the front, tried hard to control her giggle. Amit was intensely involved in his narration and continued without a break.

"Vinod and I ordered something to eat. When I saw the injured girl, she still held her bleeding thumb. I told Vinod I would be right back and left. I went back to the bus and got a Band-Aid bandage from my bag. Back in the restaurant, I walked over to the girl and gave it to her. Before they could say anything, I was back at my seat. Vinod grinned at me knowingly.

"We finished our dinner in the next fifteen minutes and boarded the bus again. After a few minutes, both the girls came back too and smiled at us before taking their seats. The injured girl thanked me with a shy smile. I grinned and said, "You are welcome!"

The moment Amit said this, Raj retorted, "You are welcome! Wow! Since when have you been so well- mannered and chivalrous? Or was this an exception?"

Everyone laughed at Raj's witty comment. This annoyed Amit. Irritated, he said, "This is why I don't want to share anything with you guys. You don't take anything seriously!"

Raj didn't want the group to lose an opportunity to pull Amit's leg so he apologized and asked him to continue with his story.

"Vinod and I talked for some more time. After half an hour, I realised that Vinod had stopped responding to me. When I looked at him, he had dozed off.

"For the next fifteen-twenty minutes, I looked out of the window. It was completely dark outside. I saw lights only when another vehicle crossed our bus in the dark. I tried to see if I could spot a milestone that could tell me how far we were from our destination but could see nothing.

Behind me, both girls were chatting away. There was a chuckling sound at regular intervals. I tried overhearing their conversation but they spoke too softly to be heard over the heavy groan of the bus engine.

"After a while, it seemed that one of the girls had also dozed off. The girl to whom I had offered a Band-Aid, also looked out of the window, like me. I decided to strike a conversation with her.

"Hi! My name is Amit and you are?"

"Hi, my name is Veena!" she replied, speaking softly.

"You live at Hyderabad?"

"Yes, I do and you?"

"I belong to Kanpur. My cousin lives at Nagpur. We are visiting Hyderabad to see its historical and cultural side. I have heard a lot about it."

"So which places can we visit there and where can we stay overnight?" I asked.

"Hyderabad is not a village! You will find many boarding options near the bus-stand or you can go to the accommodations near the railway station, where you will also find many options. There are many places to visit in Hyderabad like Salar Jung Museum and Golconda fort," she said.

I just nodded between our conversations and let her do the talking. After that our conversation continued for almost another half an hour."

"We talked about our academics, likes, dislikes and on many other topics.

She was beginning to feel sleepy. By the time she would wake up, we might reach Hyderabad and go our separate ways. It was now or never!

"May I request you to be our guide for the next couple of days?" I asked.

At first, she hesitated. After a few moments of thought, she agreed. Perhaps this was her way to thank me for helping her.

The next couple of days were exciting and fun. We were thrilled to experience a new culture, architecture, history and cuisine in the company of our lovely hosts.

Amit looked around expecting looks of appreciation from everyone. When he found no such response, he looked at Raj in mute appeal. Raj understood his wish and said, "Wow! What a great experience! You must have enjoyed a lot during your visit. Unfortunately, none of us has any such story to share. I am not sure about others but definitely, I don't have any.

Raj began to clap and everyone else followed suit. Amit was now on cloud nine.

Raj asked Amit, "How far has your story reached? I mean, did it progress any further and do we need to now go to Hyderabad in the next vacation to attend your wedding?"

Amit paled on hearing this. He looked vulnerable and embarrassed. He removed his spectacles and wiped his face with his handkerchief before he could speak any further. Everyone waited for him to speak up. He stood mute, staring at his feet, unable to speak.

He took a few sips of water and mumbled, "Raj, my story came to a full stop the moment we left Hyderabad!" There was pure agony in his voice.

Everyone was amazed, *what is he saying?* Had he proposed so early and she rejected or she already had a boyfriend and hence did not accept his proposal? There were many such notions in everyone's mind and everyone was curious to know more.

After a couple of minute's silence, Amit said, "It was my fault. She gave us her time and there were many places where we used to connect in the morning. We were so excited that we didn't share any details except our names."

Amit said in a single shot and took a deep breath. Raj hugged him and patted his back and tried to console him.

"Don't worry Amit," Raj murmured. "God must have something very special for you. That's the reason he is keeping you single, unlike most of us who have someone in our life."

When he finished, Pavani stared at him. She was surprised to hear him assume about everyone's romantic status. He should only talk about himself, how he could speak on everyone's behalf?

The recess was over and everyone left for their classes. Pavani wanted to go out to watch a movie and insisted that Vaishali accompany her. It was the last day of a Kajol-starrer. She being a diehard fan of the actor, there was no chance that she would miss the movie.

Vaishali was unable to accompany her since she had a prior commitment. The more categorically Vaishali refused, the more insistent Pavani became. Finally, Raj chimed in to resolve the deadlock. He offered to accompany Pavani for the movie. At first, Pavani dilly-dallied but her eagerness to watch the movie persuaded her to agree. She asked Raj to meet her at the college gate after ten minutes and Raj agreed.

Raj reached the gate with five minutes to spare. He checked his watch at least ten times during the next five minutes. Finally, his wait was over and Pavani too reached the gate. She looked beautiful as she had changed her top, which she had in her bag.

Her white top went well with her light blue jeans. With her silky, curly hair tumbling around her oval face, she looked stunning. Raj was bowled over. He stared at her, captivated. He seemed to have seen her for the first time. Pavani always dressed casually for college. This was the first time he was going on an outing with her. He had never seen her give so much attention to her attire before.

"I am ready to go!" she said. When he didn't respond and stood lost, she shook him out of his reverie. With a start, he apologized. Pavani smiled and they came out of the college.

* * *

Chapter - 7

It was around 11:30 in the morning when they emerged from the college. They boarded a public conveyance and reached Heer Palace, one of the best-known cinema halls among the youngsters due to its close vicinity to many famous hangouts. One could find many youngsters in the movie hall, chatting and enjoying their get-togethers.

The movie hall was crowded. Many colleges had re-opened after their semester breaks. Students were in a celebratory mood, meeting each other after a break. The long queue at the ticket window made them wonder if they would get the tickets for the upcoming matinee show.

Raj wasn't in favour of diving into the sea of movie enthusiasts to buy the tickets. He suggested they try some other movie Pavani would hear nothing of it. She was determined to watch the movie of her favourite actress. She decided to get into the ladies queue, though Raj didn't like it. He tried to express his displeasure but Pavani didn't pay heed and continued her struggle.

After fifteen minutes of an almost scuffle, she finally succeeded in getting two tickets for the movie. She waved the tickets triumphantly to Raj. She felt as if she had scaled the Everest. She was on the cloud nine and couldn't wait anymore to watch the movie.

Finally, the door of the movie hall opened and both of them grabbed their seats. The show was packed to capacity. There was a lot of noise and commotion as most of the audience was made up of college students in a boisterous, celebratory mood. Whistling, cheers and loud voices created a cacophony. After few ads and statutory warnings, the movie finally started and there was silence in the hall.

Pavani was transformed as soon as the movie began. Gone was the sombre, no-nonsense girl who had to have logical reasons for everything she did. As soon as the censor board certificate came up on the screen, signifying the start of the movie, she clapped her hands excitedly and literally bounced in her seat. Poor Raj, already captivated, was absolutely mesmerized. Pavani turned to him grinning, her eyes shining, her cheeks pink, looking happier than he had ever seen her. He couldn't help but grin in response. Her enthusiasm was infectious.

Once the movie began, however, Pavani was completely engrossed. Raj made a few attempts to start a conversation with her but she was least interested. She had been sucked into the celluloid world and had no consciousness for the real world she had left behind on the threshold. Raj had no option but to watch the movie too.

After the movie was over, Pavani was delighted as if she had won the Miss Universe title!

I think that happens with all of us; when we get something that we badly want, something which we are so fond of, be it big or small, we are ecstatic and feel on top of the world.

Ms Roy Chaudhary looked at Mrinalini and both of them smiled.

Once out of the cinema hall, Raj asked Pavani if she wanted to have a cup of coffee. She wanted to rush home and avoid spending more time with Raj. She remembered Vaishali's revelation of Raj's feelings towards herself too well. But she was obliged to accept the offer for coffee as Raj had helped her to watch a movie she so badly wanted to. Raj was euphoric but tried hard to control his emotions.

They made their way to the adjoining Kwality Restaurant. It was a famous hangout among the youth owing to its ambience, lip-smacking food and pocket-friendly menu.

The close proximity to colleges made the restaurant a great hit among youngsters. The restaurant had special arrangements to make the place suitable for intimate conversations. This made it easier to talk even when the food-joint was abuzz with activity.

Pavani and Raj reached the restaurant at around 3:15 pm. It wasn't too crowded, just a few college students. Both of them found a comfortable place in a corner to sit. It was away from the chaos and the hustle-bustle of the place.

They took their seats. When the waiter came, Raj asked Pavani if she wanted something to eat but she declined. Raj ordered two hot coffees with one sandwich.

When the waiter left, Raj decided he didn't want to lose the golden opportunity to slip from his hands. Easing into the conversation, he asked, "So Pavani, how were your holidays?"

"They were good but nothing worth mentioning like Amit's holidays."

Raj smiled and said, "So what are you planning after graduation?"

"Ummm.... I haven't thought about it yet. I am not sure what I should do, look for a government job or pursue a management degree," she said.

"Hmmm.... It is really difficult to decide about the profession you wish to choose," said Raj.

"What is your plan?" she asked him.

"I plan to prepare for CAT (Common Admission Test) for admission into a management program. I don't think I can really do a government job. Though my father wants me to take up his business, I am not keen to run our family business. I guess I am not meant for it," said Raj.

"That's great!" said Pavani. "Your thoughts are so clear. You seem to have your future course planned. I think I too need to think and be clearer about my future."

Their coffee was served. The waiter placed the coffee cups and the sandwich plate at the table and left.

Raj looked around self-consciously. When he was sure that no one seemed unduly interested in them, he continued.

"You are right," Raj said, looking into her eyes. "I am clear in my thoughts on the professional front. But on the personal front, I have many dreams which I haven't been able to turn into reality as yet."

Pavani stared at him, a little embarrassed. Sensing her discomfort, he left it at that, offered her a sandwich and asked her to have the coffee. He picked up his own cup too and took a few sips of it.

After a couple of minutes' silence, when he saw that she was comfortable again, he broached the topic again.

"Pavani, I'm sure you have guessed what I am about to say. I know that Vaishali has told you how I feel about you. However, I would like to tell you myself, even though I don't have eloquent words to speak. I am not usually expressive about my feelings, as you well know. Even so, I can no longer keep my feelings to myself. I want to tell you everything and know what your answer is!"

Pavani became intensely nervous. This was the last thing she expected. It was all too sudden and overwhelming. She fought hard to control her reactions.

She didn't want to lose a good friend, which she feared she might if she blurted something out thoughtlessly.

"Raj," she said after a pause, "I am not sure what you want to discuss. I am not sure what Vaishali said the other day... or the point she was trying to make. I am not sure how will I react to anything you say. Right now, I do not want to discuss anything!"

After saying that, she put her cup down, picked up her bag and left before Raj could react or stop her.

Raj stared at the glass door of the restaurant that Pavani had exited from in the blink of an eye. Raj wasn't sure if he had timed such a serious discussion right. This was certainly an unexpected outcome.

Raj felt morose. *Have I blown my chance? He asked himself.*

* * *

Chapter - 8

From that day on, Pavani began to avoid Raj. The more he tried to talk to her, the most distant she became. She thwarted all his plans and averted any situation in which she had to face him.

Vaishali could see the friction between Raj and Pavani. She felt responsible somehow. She was sure she could diffuse the situation between these two important members of the most active group in the college.

She decided to tackle Raj first. She tried to ask him the reason for the widening gap between the two of them. Raj tried his best to hide, insisting there was no gap. But couldn't continue with his fake stories and pseudo expressions in front of Vaishali's insistence and shared the entire incident.

Vaishali had suspected the reason and now it was clear. She placed her hands on his shoulders and patted him, trying her best to console him. She could hear the despondency in his voice. His eyes glittered as he blinked away his sadness. He told Vaishali that he seems to have lost the battle even before fighting it. Vaishali promised to work something out and make sure that their relationship isn't torn off the tree by the storm, even before it is ripened. She beseeched him to be of good heart and not give up.

Next week was Vaishali's birthday. She was very excited because, after endless entreaties, her parents had finally given her permission to throw a party for her birthday. Excited, she had invited all her friends to her house. She had planned lots of games and activities to make the party exciting and memorable. Usually, she would ask Pavani for help but this time she asked Amit to help her. She had a plan which she wanted to keep secret from Pavani. At last, her birthday arrived!

On the morning of her birthday, her mother made her favourite dish for breakfast-*Poha*. Her father went to the famous nearby sweet-shop to buy some hot, crispy *Jalebis* and *Khurchan*. Her brother picked up a variety of flowers to decorate the drawing room before she got up in the morning.

Her mother also invited Pavani to be there for the whole day to help her in all the preparations. Although everything was almost done yet an extra helping hand was always better.

As decided, Pavani was there at 8 am sharp. She was as punctual as a clock. Vaishali's mother opened the door and found her with a small bag with some gifts and a dress for the evening party. She smiled and welcomed Pavani.

"Good morning, *Aunty*!" Pavani greeted.

"Good Morning, *Beta*. Please come in!" Vaishali's mother answered affectionately and made way for her.

Pavani came in the drawing room and was awe-struck by the decorations. She asked, "Where is Vaishali? Is she still sleeping? Nice decoration! Who did it?"

"It is by Baua. He was busy since morning. Your uncle brought Vaishali's favourite sweets in the morning." She answered and looked at both Vaishali's father and brother who also sat in the drawing room.

Pavani smiled and greeted them both. Vaishali's mother asked her to sit in the drawing room and have a cup of tea. Pavani nodded.

She sat down on the sofa. Vaishali's father was sitting on the other sofa, reading the newspaper. Pavani wanted to meet her friend and wish her first, but Vaishali's room was closed. She looked around for something to do while she waited. There was nothing to engage her attention except for the decoration Vaishali's brother had done. Now that she paid attention to it, Baua had really done an excellent job.

Vaishali's mom brought tea and cookies for everyone. The new crockery set was taken out of the cupboard and was to be used to serve all the guests for the day. Vaishali's mother was proud to showcase her treasure of crockery, which she got a chance to flaunt after many months.

It was a nice white colour gold trimmed Noritake Crockery set. A new Bamboo tray had white cups with saucer and a plate with biscuits. Unfortunately, the birthday girl was not present at the moment and Pavani got all the attention Vaishali should have got.

Vaishali's father folded the newspaper and looked at the tray.

"Hmmm.... So Pavani looks like we all are getting the royal treatment today! Hahaha!" he guffawed.

Everyone laughed in response. Pavani looked at Vaishali's door wishing it open.

Vaishali's father noticed her look and suggested, "It seems the birthday girl needs royal treatment in her own room. Pavani, why don't you take the tray to her room?"

He looked at Pavani and smiled.

Pavani handed out their tea to Vaishali's parents and brother and took the remaining two cups to Vaishali's room. The walls of the corridor leading to Vaishali's room were beautifully decorated with coloured paper streamers and fresh flowers. There were few butterflies and lanterns on the ceiling. It looked so festive and bright that Pavani found herself wishing that she also had a sibling who could pamper her. She reached Vaishali's room and pushed the door open.

As always, Vaishali's room was a mess. Her table was full of books and loose paper sheets on which some notes were randomly scribbled.

Pavani looked around wondering when Vaishali would grow up. Vaishali was fast asleep. Since the room was at the farthest corner of the house, there was no sound from outside. The only sound in the room was from the ceiling fan.

Holding the tray in one hand, Pavani made some space on the study table to keep the tray before trying to wake Vaishali up. Then she tried to pull off the sheet Vaishali was curled up under. The moment she sensed someone was trying to pull it off, Vaishali pulled it up to cover her face. Pavani couldn't pull the sheet off. Changing tactics, she began to tickle Vaishali with both hands. For the next few seconds, it was a battle between the two girls, where Vaishali was trying to protect herself and Pavani was not letting her do so. Finally, Vaishali woke up.

Pavani hugged Vaishali tightly and wished her.

"Wish you a very happy birthday, my dear! May God bless you and keep you happy always!"

"Thank you so much Pavani! You know Pavani, before falling asleep last night, I wanted you to be the first one to wish me. And see, my wish has been fulfilled. Looks like my lucky day today. If I'd asked for more, I'm sure I'd have got it too!"

"Where is my gift?" demanded Vaishali with the right of a friend.

Pavani smiled and pointed her finger towards the tea-tray and said, "You will definitely get a gift from me, but before that let's have a cup of tea."

Vaishali nodded and told her that she'll be right back from the washroom.

Pavani started looking around her room. The room too was decorated as the rest of the house. She admired the work of Vaishali's brother. He must have decorated the room after Vaishali fell asleep. It seemed that he did it all in absolute silence, without disturbing her. She smiled to herself at the thought but was gloomy the very next moment. She thought- *why hasn't God given me a sibling? Why is she devoid of experiencing such a great relationship and bonding?* She heard many stories from Vaishali about her brother. She recalled a few lines from a skit she had played in school.

We love, We fight!

We feel proud, We envy!

We support, We differ!

But whenever someone else tries to talk against any of us, we are always together.

And whenever we have any reason to celebrate, we are together.

Yes, we are siblings!

The more she thought about it, the more depressed she became. Suddenly, she was hugged from behind while she was lost in her thoughts. Vaishali was back. Pavani turned around and smiled, "Vaishali, you are my best friend and it is your birthday today! Trust me, I wish you the best of everything life has. But for the first time since I have known you, I am jealous of you!"

Vaishali was stunned at Pavani's sombre words.

Pavani continued to talk. "Look around your room and the entire house! Your brother has taken such pains to make your day special! I am sure you feel immensely loved. I wish I too had something like that. I wish I too had a sibling."

After saying this, Pavani turned away, hiding her tear from her friend. Vaishali sensed her loneliness. She took that as a blessing in disguise and said, "Cheer up, girl! Today is my birthday! I am as good as a sibling to you. Why are you thinking morbid thoughts and making yourself sad? We are sisters and friends too!"

She grinned and Pavani cheered up too. "But you don't fight with me," she said with a pout. "I have heard that non-fighting siblings are like distant relatives."

"Okay, *Baba.* I will now fight with you every now and then and make sure you don't feel lonely because of not having any sibling. I am your sibling as of this moment. And one should always listen to sibling advice. Today is my day so you can't refuse anything I say but before I say anything, let's have tea as I am feeling sleepy without it!" declared Vaishali.

As soon as they finished with their tea, Vaishali asked, "Where is my gift?"

"Oh no! I forgot to bring it!" Pavani replied, a twinkle in her eyes.

"Don't try to fool me! I know you must have brought some gift for me. Where is it?" Vaishali looked around to find her gift.

"You are right. I did bring you a gift. I kept it somewhere on the table and now I can't find it because the table is such a mess. Can you please help me find it?"

Vaishali gave her an annoyed look and started searching for her gift. She quickly kept the books and papers back in their places. The table was cleared up in a jiffy but Vaishali still did not find her gift.

Pavani was smiling to herself at having successfully tricked Vaishali to clear up her room. In ten minutes, the room was neat. Books were stacked properly; loose papers were put in a folder; the bed was made and the bedspread was wrinkle free. Everything was cleaned but Vaishali could not find her gift. She angrily looked at Pavani. Pavani also understood the gravity of the situation and eagerness of Vaishali so without making her wait anymore, she slowly pulled her mattress from one corner and picked up a small gift-wrapped box. With a squeal of delight, Vaishali snatched it from Pavani and opened it. It was a shining silver chain with a beautifully filigreed locket with the letter 'V' woven in it.

She hugged Pavani and immediately went to the mirror in the corner of her room. She adorned the beautiful neckpiece and checked herself out.

It was obvious that she loved her gift. Vaishali caught hold of Pavani's hands a spun her around happily.

"Stop! Stop! Stop!" Pavani said in a tizzy. "Where is my return gift?"

"You are my best friend so you will get the best return gift from me," said Vaishali with a mischievous smirk.

Pavani stared at her with a suspicious look. "Where is it?" she demanded.

"You'll get it in the evening," Vaishali said, grinning.

"But I gave you the birthday gift right now so why should I wait till evening for my gift?" she asked.

Vaishali smiled at her and shrugged her shoulders. Her smile was mysterious; Pavani couldn't decipher it. She didn't have a choice but to wait until evening.

Chapter - 9

The terrace of Vaishali's home was transformed into a party hub by Baua. There was a temporary structure on the terrace roofed with cement sheets. It was approximately fifteen feet by twenty feet, covered on three sides and open on the fourth. Baua had left no stone unturned to deck up the terrace with lights and flowers.

There were a couple of large linen-covered tables on one side for serving the food. The chairs were on the other side. In the middle, there was a small beautifully decorated round-table meant for cake-cutting.

Amit and Raj were the first ones to reach in the evening, well before the party was to begin. Both of them wanted to spend time with Vaishali before the rest of the guests arrived.

After reaching there and wishing Vaishali, Amit went straight to the terrace to help Baua. After talking to him for a couple of minutes, he started the decoration with him. Raj and Pavani too reached there but Amit told them to relax as he could alone take up the remaining work with Baua. Both of them sat in a corner on of the chairs laid for the party.

Things had normalized between them to a large extent. But not all the way. The earlier bonhomie was missing. Pavani no longer laughed as easily as she did once. Raj too was guarded in his speech.

He had always loved to tease Pavani. A sure-shot way to raise her heckles was to say something uncomplimentary about Kajol and then counter all the arguments that she gave. They both enjoyed the banter that sprang up between them as a result. Now, the mention of Kajol was sure to remind her of the unpleasant incident that had soured things between them. Naturally, he didn't want to remind her of that day.

It was a beautiful evening. The sun was about to set. The sky had turned orange and the breeze was getting cooler. Birds were flying back to their nests and the chirping of birds on the Neem tree next to Vaishali's house filled the atmosphere.

They sat together for a while, neither of them saying a word. Raj could see that Pavani was not interested in any conversation. Disappointed, he got up stood by the parapet wall looking out towards the road. Pavani also got up and went to Vaishali's room to get ready for the party.

Amit was busy helping Baua. Raj noticed a large net hamper filled with inflated balloons. Assuming the balloons were to be used for decoration, he asked Amit how they were to be put up.

“Oh, those balloons aren’t for decoration,” he said mysteriously. He refused to answer any more of Raj’s questions. Raj knew Amit had been secretly planning something with Vaishali for a couple of weeks but was not aware what exactly it was.

Around 6 pm, all the college friends started pouring in for the party. Baua and some of his friends took the responsibility of receiving the guests and serving the starters. Meanwhile, Vaishali’s mother took charge for the dinner with a cook they had engaged for the evening.

They started serving Mango *Lassi* with wafers to all the guests. Everyone mingled and enjoyed the evening.

Vaishali and Pavani were at the terrace to greet all the friends coming for the party. Vaishali was in her flared and ruffled dress in plain white georgette. The skirt of the dress fell to her feet in sculpted folds. Her silver tipped open-toed stilettoes peeped from under the hem, giving her a dreamy, angelic appearance. Pavani was dressed beautifully in a sequinned pink t-shirt paired with stone-washed blue denim.

Vaishali looked stunning and everyone who wished her couldn’t help but notice her beauty and her glowing face. Vaishali was elated and greeted the guests with great enthusiasm.

Pavani’s outfit seemed too casual for the occasion, in contrast. But that was Pavani-simple and sober. Raj loved her simplicity. She was not like other girls. She had her own sense of style. Her style pertained not to attire alone but to the way she conducted herself. She was always honest and forthright with everyone. Deceit and pretence were foreign to her. She never compromised on her principles and that made her stand her out from the crowd of all the girls of her age. These character traits were enough to make Raj swoon over her.

While everyone looked at Vaishali, Pavani was the centre of attraction for Raj. He tried to hide from others while he stared at her moving around among the party guests.

After sometime Baua called his parents for the cake cutting and after that few pictures were clicked. After the pictures were clicked, everyone began drifting away, but Vaishali called for attention. It looked like she had an announcement to make.

"Friends! Thanks for coming and joining me to make my day even more special and memorable! I have a surprise for all of you. We have organized a game with the help of Amit. Thanks for all your help, Amit!"

Vaishali looked at Amit and he smiled. Vaishali continued.

"So we are going to organize a game. This game will be played by all the boys first and then the girls will play it," she said, clapping in excitement.

Pavani was surprised. She had not known about this game. She stared at Vaishali but Vaishali ignored her. It seemed that she didn't want to give Pavani any explanation at that moment.

Amit picked out four balloons from the net hamper. He gave two blue balloons to Vaishali and tied two white balloons to his own ankles. Vaishali also did the same.

After tying the balloons both stood up.

"So friends," said Amit, "the game is that others will try to stamp on your balloons and burst them and you have to protect yourself while trying to stamp on the balloons of others. If your balloons are popped, you'll be out of the game. The winner would be the person who has at least one balloon intact. Then the winner will be given a surprise task to perform. We didn't want to mix the boys and girls for this game to avoid any injuries and chaos. Therefore, it is either all the boys or all the girls.

"First Vaishali and I will play this game. If Vaishali wins, boys will play the game first and if I win, girls will play it. So are you all ready? Baua will now count to three and we will start."

Amit signalled to Baua and all the boys and girls made a circle around them. Amit and Vaishali also started moving in a circle. Both of them were very attentive and kept an eye on each other they tried to keep their legs bit back to avoid any attack from the opponent.

Baua started counting.

"O-O-One..., T-T-Two..., and Th-Th-Three........"

The moment he said THREE, both of them aimed at each other's balloons. Amit made a few solid attacks but could not burst Vaishali's balloons. Vaishali was more defensive than offensive. The girls supported Amit and boys were with Vaishali.

After receding few steps, Vaishali attacked one of Amit's balloons and burst it. The boys' excitement skyrocketed and they now shouted for Vaishali and supported her with increased fervour. Amit had the girls' support and they also cheered and shouted for him.

Finally, Vaishali played her masterstroke. She stood still for a moment and suddenly hit Amit's left ankles at lightning speed. The balloon tied to it burst! The boys whooped in joy. They clapped and high fived each other. Vaishali also jumped up and down and shouted "Y-Y-Yeeessss!" Amit went down on his knees, holding his head in both his hands in dejection.

Vaishali started dancing with excitement and all the boys went "Vaishali..... Vaishali." Now it was the turn of all the boys to play the game. All the boys came forward and tied the balloon to their ankles.

After tying the balloons, all the boys were ready for the battle and just waited for a final nod. Amit gave Vaishali's balloons to Raj.

Finally, the battle began! The girls made a circle and the boys played in the middle. Some of them tried to hide, while others were in attack mode. The ones on attack mode got kicked out first as they got attached in return.

Everyone who got out had some complaint or the other. Some got hurt, some were hopping about trying to keep their trousers clean, some hadn't understood the game. Those out of the game early were dejected. But the game continued without loss of momentum.

Raj tried to understand the game first so initially, he was on defensive mode. He quickly figured out a few tricks from the mistakes others had made. Then he went into attack mode.

Within some time, only the top three boys remained in the balloon battle. Raj was also among them. After few hits and trials, Raj won the game. He was thrilled.

Everyone cheered for him. Raj bowed and thanked everyone. Amit walked up to Raj with a small box in his hands.

He held an imaginary mike in his hands and acted as if interviewing the winner, as the captain of winning team interviews in an international match. Raj played along with the elaborate interview.

"So, Mr Raj, how are you feeling after winning this game on such a wonderful evening?"

Everyone shouted and cheered.

"It is really a wonderful evening. I think today is a great day. I didn't think I could win the game but with the grace of God and wishes from all my friends, I won! I am really excited. I think I should make a career out of this." The guests had a hearty laugh at this witty answer from Raj.

"Do you think that the wind has played an important role as you were standing in the east and wind was blowing west to east? Did this help you?"

"I think that the weather was in my favour. I prayed to God because this game is a life changer for me so I needed to win. God favoured and blessed me with a win."

Amit took a deep breath and said, "Indeed! Indeed! God was definitely with you. Now, we have a surprise gift for the winner."

Everyone looked at Amit. Pavani turned to Vaishali, with murder in her eyes. She knew there was something afoot. She glared at her and promised herself to teach her friend a lesson. *After all, I am your friend. How could you not tell me all this before?* Vaishali ignores Pavani's *I-will-kill-you* looks.

Amit opened the box and it had many folded slips of paper. Amit showed it to all and covered the box and shook it so as to mix up the slips. He removed the lid and said, "So Mr Raj, here is the surprise. You need to pull one chit from this box and read it out loud. After that, you have to do whatever is written on it."

Raj frowned for a fleeting moment. He wasn't sure what they wanted him to do. Everyone around him was still cheering so he grinned and nodded.

He picked up a chit. Before he could open it and read it out, Amit snatched it from him. He then closed the box and threw it to Baua who caught it readily. The moment his hand was free, Amit again held his imaginary mike to Raj.

"Mr Raj, what do you think, you have got in this chit? Any guesses?"

"Not really but I hope you don't ask me to do anything funny or embarrassing."

The curiosity to know Raj's secret task was palpable. Vaishali came forward and took the slip from Amit, opened it slowly and looked around before reading it out. Everyone looked at her as if she was about to announce the exam results. She cleared her throat and began to read.

"So Raj, here is what you have to do today. You have to enact a romantic scene today. Choose any girl in a pink outfit and propose to her in true Shahrukh Khan style!"

There were claps and whistles all around.

Raj blushed and took a deep breath. But he was game for the task. He looked around to see which girls were wearing pink. His eyes stopped at Pavani. Pavani tried to hide behind some girls. She was embarrassed and nervous. Her face had turned pink, like her top. She hadn't suspected anything like this happening.

Vaishali used to share each and everything with her then how come she planned such a big thing planned and didn't even inform her? Though Amit met her regularly, he too hadn't shared this plan. She cursed herself for being too dumb to sense what was cooking.

Yes, this was pre-planned and Vaishali is the mastermind behind all this. I will definitely kill her. How she could do this to me? She has really put me in fix. She is not my best friend. Had she been one, she could have at least discussed her hidden plan with me. Why she had to create such a fuss in front of so many people and put me in an embarrassing situation? She is bad, very bad. I won't talk to her anymore! Pavani soliloquized, deeply mortified.

Oh, God! Please help me. Please hide me somewhere. I do not want to be a part of this game now. Had I known it before, I would have never joined this party. Raj, please stop staring at me. There are so many other girls who are also in pink. Why can't you choose them and leave me?

Raj's stare at Pavani prompted Vaishali to pull Pavani to the centre of the circle. Leaving her there, facing Raj, Vaishali stepped back into the circle others had made around them.

Everyone began cheering. Pavani was unable to look around. Her eyes were fixed on the floor. Her mind had suddenly turned into a spider's web. Thoughts and feelings entangled in her mind.

Raj couldn't take his eyes off Pavani. She still hoped for a miracle that would help her run away, far from this extremely embarrassing situation. He moved closer to her and went down on his knees. He looked up into her eyes but she refused to meet his eyes. Her heart was beating like a trip-hammer. The party began to clap. Their excitement was high, heavy with anticipation.

The atmosphere was just perfect for the proposal. The sun had set in its western home and the sky was prodigiously orange-red, turning the evening perfectly romantic. The bird-song was hushed. A slight breeze had picked up, giving a dreamy feel to the whole set. Pavani felt goosebumps all the way from her feet to her scalp. Though she had tied her hair in a ponytail, a few hair strands managed to escape and partially covered her face.

When Raj tried to hold her hands, she snatched them away to brush her hair away from her face. It didn't do any good. The hair was back, playing over her dewy face again.

Raj knew this was the moment to seize. If he couldn't do it now, he would regret it for his whole life. He held Pavani's hands firmly in his without giving her a chance to snatch them away. Pavani froze and didn't know how to react. She knew there was no running away now.

Of course, she could have pulled her hands away. But this time she didn't even try. It seemed as if she had given up the struggle and surrendered to the moment. Her heart still pounded heavily, filling her ears with it. She couldn't hear any other sound.

When Raj held her hand, he could feel her heartbeats. His heart was pounding too. The veins in their hands filled with blood and throbbed in unison.

Teenage is the most glorious phase of life. Each moment is intensely alive, filled to the brim with larger-than-life sensations. There are new umpteen experiences to savour for the first time. The raging roller-coaster of emotions heightens each experience multi-fold.

The first day of college; first girlfriend or boyfriend; the first crush; the first love. Opening your heart out to someone for the first time or hearing someone say something special for the first time-all such experiences make this phase unlike any other. The thrill of exploring life for the first time is a powerful and heady feeling. This is exactly what Pavani and Raj were experiencing at that moment.

The guests were busy cheering for them and whistling out of excitement because for them it was a game. But there were many things that went inside Pavani and Raj's mind; something only they could understand and no one else. It was not a game for them anymore.

Raj gently kissed Pavani's hand. Pavani was shy and bashful. She tried to pull her hands away but couldn't. Raj held them firmly, both in his mind and his grip.

Raj looked into her eyes. He noted that her nervousness and embarrassment had taken a back seat. He took a deep breath and gently caressed her hand.

"Pavani, I am not sure what you think about me. I know you think of me as a friend. I appreciate your trust in me. I also know you are very concerned about other people. But Pavani, this is our life and we have to think about ourselves," he said gently.

"The first day when we met, we had a terrible fight. When I reached home that evening, I thought about you. I rebuked myself for being so discourteous. I recalled your shocked look. When I met you the next day, I shocked myself by being unforgivably rude to you once more. I couldn't understand why I was being nasty. That was not my nature! By the time the week ended, I knew, I had fallen madly in love with you. I had no idea how to handle the deluge of emotions. I told myself I was being stupid. To stop myself from blurting out how I felt about you, I had behaved badly. I know it was dumb of me. Can you forgive me?"

Raj's voice cracked and he felt a lump in his throat. His eyes were moist. For the two of them, everyone else had vanished. They were with each other, that is all they knew. Raj paused, overwhelmed. Pavani stood with her head lowered. He couldn't see her face or he'd have seen that her eyes had filled up too.

"When I understood what my feelings were, I started observing you closely so that I could understand you. The more I studied you, deeper I loved you. Your voice and words were melodious to me like the early morning birdsong. Your presence was like drops of rain that fall on the grass and makes it glitter like diamonds."

Pavani stood still. She heard everything but didn't react. This didn't deter Raj.

"After a few months, I knew that you are the girl for me. You are in my thoughts every moment. No matter what I do, I feel as if you are watching me lovingly. You have become the voice in my head, guiding me at all times. If I am about to do something that I feel you will not appreciate, I don't do it. Even if you would never know about it. Every cell in my body is intensely aware of you- whether you are with me or not. I want to be with you every moment of every day and I know this will not change. Yes, Pavani, I love you. I never want to lose you, ever. I love you with all my heart and soul. It is not possible that you don't feel the same. You have inspired such deep love in me, surely you cannot be unaffected? You are the angel of my life, my heart. Confess now, do you not love me too?"

Everyone started clapping like crazy and now everyone moved towards Pavani and started cheering her to respond. Though she was hesitant but no one was allowing her to go out without responding to the proposal of Raj. Raj waited anxiously for her to reply. The whole party was hushed as everyone waited. Raj held Pavani's hand firmly. Her heartbeats raced like a racer on the F1 track and her cheeks were wet. The moment, Raj finished it.

The truth was, she had known how Raj felt about her, even before Vaishali had told her. She had known because for the past few months she too had realized that she was happy only when Raj was around. His absence made her feel lost and hollow. She had fallen in love with Raj, as completely as he had. She was sure a part of him had known that just as she had known that he cared for her.

She knew Raj would surely propose to her someday but she had not anticipated that the day would come so soon. She was content to wait until they had both made something of their lives. Until then, as far as she was concerned, the unsaid could remain unsaid. Yet, a part of her ached to hear the words Raj had just spoken. She desperately wanted to hear them. A girl in love would surely want to be told that her love was reciprocated.

She knew she would readily accept Raj the day he pronounced those sweet words. At last, the unsaid had been said! Her heart danced with relief and joy! She hadn't dared to hope that this day would come so soon!

She knelt down and held both of Raj's hands in hers, looking into his eyes. All her shyness has disappeared. Other people did not exist, only Raj did.

She looked deep into his eyes. Her eyes shone like stars; her smile was pure joy. All this while at the party she was aloof. This was the return gift Vaishali had planned for her. How well Vaishali knew her! She was an angel and the truest friend anyone could want!

She took a deep breath and began talking.

"Raj, I have heard that when one sincerely loves someone, the whole universe conspires to unite them. It seems to have worked that day for us, hasn't it?

"The only difference between us is that I didn't realize my feelings for you as quickly as you did. It took me many months to know how I felt. Nevertheless, my love is as deep as yours is, today.

"I have seen the way you ease things out for everyone. You are always ready to help people. You are dependable and responsible. Your loyalty and support mean a lot to people. Being the modest person you are, you have probably not realized how people seek you to discuss their challenges. Your advice is valuable to them because you think things through before you suggest anything.

"I love your attitude of taking things as they come. You know which matters to take seriously and which don't deserve much attention. You are easy-going and naturally cheerful. You inspire me and that fills me with even more affection for you. I didn't realise when my like converted into affection and love for you."

Pavani took a pause and continued.

"When I don't see you in college, I feel anxious and upset. Nothing seems to work, nothing is interesting. Your presence gives colour to my most ordinary moments and makes them glow. I just want to know you are there. I know I can relax and not worry about a thing. As long as you are around, no harm can reach me. You are my protective shield and armour. In the beginning, I considered you my best friend. Now I have realised that you are not just a friend but a lot more.

"Raj, I love you. You are my lifeline. I want to be with you every moment. I can't imagine a day without you. Promise me you will always be with me and never leave me alone! You will be there with me even when no one else is."

Overwhelmed, Raj nodded and put his arms around her and held her close.

Everybody burst into cheers!

* * *

Chapter - 10

That night Pavani could not sleep.

The joy of first love made her restless and kept her awake. The intoxicating fragrance of first love filled her like the aroma of wet earth after the first shower of rain. Her ears were filled with the sound of love knocking on the door of a teenager's heart.

Next day morning, when she got up, it wasn't the same day like other days. It was pretty different for her. That morning was seeming very beautiful. She could hear the melodious orchestra sound from the chirping of the birds mixed with the bustling of the moths despite the noisy vehicle sound mixed in it.

She opened the window of her room and looked outside her mini-garden. The orange rays of the Sun were lying on the multi-coloured flowers and the dewdrops were looking splendid and glittering like pearls. Vibrant Butterflies were making the entire environment like gorgeous scenic morning.

She never experienced such a vivid morning in her life. It seemed to be an effect of her first love that she was experiencing the morning more stunning and different from others or she started seeing the beautiful colours of the Mother Nature which was never experienced by her till now.

She was looking very blissful today. She reached near to the mirror and saw herself. She was blushing, she tried to cover her face from her hands and closed her eyes.

She slowly removed her hands from her face. Her eyes were still closed. She slowly opened her eyes and saw herself in the mirror again. She could see the glow in her face, she could feel the vibrating heartbeat inside her, she could find so many thoughts going in her mind. She looked at the mirror again and smiled.

For the first time in her life, she realized how beautiful she was? She wondered why she was always too shy to admit that to herself. She declared herself beautiful, heavenly and one in a million. She grinned happily, twirling around.

Her happy thoughts turned her face pink, shyly.

When she looked at the clock, she realized that she was getting now late to college so she ran to get ready.

After scanning through her entire wardrobe, she couldn't find anything which she could wear that day. Finally, she selected an off-white pair of jeans and a pink top. She tied her hair loosely with a clip. Wisps of hair escaped from the clip and played across her face.

On the way to college, she felt as if everyone was looking at her. Her sensibilities were in such a pitch that day that she blushed at eye contact. Her eyes bore testimony to the confusions of her inner being.

When she reached college, she was very excited. She was going to meet Raj for the first time after he proposed to her yesterday. Though she was excited, she was also nervous. Her heart was thumping. She wanted to spend some quality time with Raj, where no one could disturb them and they would be all by themselves. She wanted to live that moment fully.

To find such a place was not possible in college. She decided to skip college and go for an outing with Raj. She was hesitant about asking Raj out for a date but she really wanted to spend time with him. She wanted to be with him in a cosy place where they could share a conversation, their feelings or even silence.

She knew Raj's proposal was genuine but a tiny part of her wondered if it had been just a game. The thought agitated her. She couldn't bear the doubt. She had painted too many dreams of their life together in the past few hours.

When she saw Vaishali, she waved to her. Vaishali gave her a happy grin, delighted that her plan had worked. She wanted to see Raj and Pavani together and now she would! She gave Pavani a big hug and happily twirled her around a few times. Pavani laughed, a little surprised at her child-like excitement. She knew Vaishali was happy for her and this was her way of celebrating it. She really was the best friend Pavani could have asked for.

In the next few minutes, Raj and Amit joined them. She greeted them with a soft smile. Though both were standing next to her and she continued to talk to Vaishali, her eyes were only for Raj. He dominated all her attention. She tried not to stare at him but knew she was doing exactly that.

Each eye contact with Raj sent her heartbeats racing. She hoped nobody else could hear her heart beating. She was grateful for the noisy college environment else it would have been really difficult for her to hide her eagerness.

It was not just Pavani who was eager to meet Raj today. Raj was equally impatient. While Pavani was trying to control her feelings, Raj had already begged Vaishali to arrange another meeting with Pavani.

Vaishali took Pavani to the washroom which was a little away from the noise and bustle of the place where they were standing.

The washroom was a bit deserted this early in the morning. Vaishali stopped Pavani and held both her hands firmly.

"Pavani, you are looking beautiful. Your eyes are speaking volumes. There is an ocean of love in them. You can drive anyone crazy today. Trust me, even I would have wanted to date you if I were a boy," she said, giggling.

"Pavani, are you not happy?"

Pavani had not expected the question. Surprised, she said, "No, I am very happy! What makes you ask this?"

"I want to see my friend happy. I know you love Raj and so does he. I don't know why you were trying to hide your feelings. If you feel that he is the one for you, why are you shying away?

Both of you share such a great understanding! I am sure with time your bond will grow stronger.

"I think, both of you should spend some time together and understand each other. Talk about everything you have in your heart or mind. Love is a fragile plant. It needs the support of mature understanding and honest communication to make it sturdy."

Pavani nodded. "You are right, Vaishali! I too want to spend time with Raj. There is so much to talk about, so many things to clarify. But how do we find the time? We have a full day of classes today and the same schedule over the next few days!"

"You are saying this!" asked an incredulous Vaishali. "A girl who is always ready to bunk classes to watch Kajol's movie! You don't think twice when you want to watch a movie but today you are worried about classes? People say love brings maturity. Looks like my friend has matured in less than twenty-four hours!

"Your life is more important than a couple of classes. I will help both of you with notes but right now it is important that both of you should spend time together."

Pavani nodded.

"That's like a good girl," said Vaishali approvingly. "But now, no more class bunking for Kajol, okay?"

Pavani grinned impudently.

"Go to some quiet place and have a talk today," advised Vaishali.

"I want to, but will Raj agree?" Pavani questioned.

"Yes, he will. He told me he wants to spend time with you today," Vaishali said.

Raj and Amit were anxiously waiting in the corridor. Vaishali nodded to the anxious Raj and he grinned happily. Soon both Pavani and Raj were out of the college, walking towards Phool Bagh.

Phool Bagh was barely a fifteen-minute walk from their college. Walking together, Pavani and Raj were silent but were intensely conscious of the other.

Ganesh Shankar Vidyarthi Udyan or Phool Bagh is one of the oldest gardens of Kanpur. In the reign of Queen Victoria, it was known as Queen Victoria Garden. This garden has been used for many political gatherings. It has various varieties of rare plants and trees. It is a well-maintained place with new landscaped features added to it recently.

Raj found a bench under the shade of dense trees so that they both were protected from the overhead sun. Pavani liked the place and they sat down.

They looked around, avoiding each other's eyes. They were both waiting for the other to initiate conversation. Their hesitancy was natural since this was their first meeting after the emotionally charged proposal.

Raj took Pavani's hand in his and caressed it gently. When he did not say anything, Pavani asked, "Are we going to sit here holding hands like this or are we going to talk?"

"Why don't you say something?" asked Raj, smiling.

"Alright then, I will talk. Raj, I hope, we are doing the right thing. I hope, we are not making a mistake we might regret. I hope our families will support our relationship."

Pavani's question was genuine. Raj knew that it might not be so easy to convince his orthodox parents. His father was very traditional but he was sure that he would be able to sort everything out.

He had very loving parents and being the only son, he was sure he would be able to convince them sooner or later.

"I am sure we are doing the right thing Pavani. My parents are pretty traditional so we might run into difficulties. But I am confident we will win through all challenges. After all, you are a wonderful girl. They would be proud and happy to have you as their daughter-in-law.

"You genuinely care for people. I have seen you go out of your way to make things easy for others. You are sensible and sensitive; mature and responsible. I have never seen you overwhelmed by anything. Your confidence and sharpness of mind are a delight to me. I haven't met anyone like you. I am so lucky that you have chosen me. Thank you! You bless my life!"

Pavani was delirious with happiness to hear him praise her.

"Raj, what else do you like about me?" she asked, hungry for more.

"Where do I begin? I love your dark, deep eyes. They are like glowing, limpid pools I want to wade to the bottom of. Your lips are so perfectly shaped! When you talk, the way your lips frame the words makes them even more enticing. Your cascade of curly hair makes me want to bury my face in it."

Pavani hadn't expected such eloquence from Raj. Her cheeks flaming, she buried her face in her hands.

"Why are you feeling shy, Pavani? Look at yourself through my eyes. You don't just have a beautiful face; your heart is as lovely. I always want to sit next to you and keep listening to you," said Raj fervently.

"Raj, your words are music to my ears. To hear you praise me is the sweetest thing on earth. But we must talk about our future! What are your plans for your masters degree? Do you still want to pursue a masters in management?"

Raj nodded. "And you?" he asked.

Pavani also nodded.

"That's great, we will support each other to study and crack CAT exam. Wouldn't it be wonderful if we get the same college?" Raj said.

They talked together almost until evening that day. They shared many things they had never shared with anyone before. They planned their future, a future filled with happiness and joy for them and their families.

For the next few weeks, Raj and Pavani were always on the look-out for finding time to spend together. Every passing day, the bond between them got stronger.

Chapter - 11

It was few days after Diwali. Raj's parents were out to attend a marriage in Aligarh and Raj was alone at home for a couple of days.

It was Raj's birthday that day. Pavani had ordered a cake for him. She collected in the morning on the way to the college. She intended to have him cut the cake in the college canteen.

When she reached, she couldn't find Raj anywhere. Amit told her that Raj was unwell so had taken a day off.

Impulsively, Pavani decided to visit Raj with the cake. She asked Vaishali to accompany her but Vaishali had a task to finish for the HOD and couldn't go. Pavani decided to go alone.

After attending the first two lectures with Vaishali, Pavani took a rickshaw and reached Raj's house. Raj's house was in Swarup Nagar. It is one of the poshest localities of Kanpur. It has wide lanes and modern, well-designed houses on both sides of the road. If one wants to find affluent residents in Kanpur, this is the area to visit.

Raj was unwell. He hadn't expected anyone, least of all Pavani. His pleased surprise gladdened Pavani. He kept on looking her for few moments when Pavani broke the silence.

"Will you not allow me inside? If this is how you are behaving already, who knows how you'll behave later!" she said, chuckling.

Raj moved aside in a hurry to let her enter. Pavani entered the large drawing room. It had a heavy three-seater teak-wood sofa on one side, a coffee table in the middle and two single seaters on the other side. There were other chairs and ottomans all over the imposing room. The room was pretty big but looked well-filled.

Raj asked her to sit. She sat on the three seater sofa. Raj sat down next to her. Pavani touched his hand to see if he still had a fever.

"How are you now?" She asked.

"I had a fever and a headache but now that you are here, I am perfectly fine," he said, smiling.

Smiling back at him, Pavani asked him to show her around his house. Raj promptly took her on a tour.

After the tour, Pavani went into the kitchen and brought a plate. She took out the cake box from its box and placed it on the plate and lit a candle on it.

While she was doing all this, Raj was looking at her quietly, mesmerized. He hadn't expected her thoughtfulness.

Raj blew the candle out as Pavani sang "Happy Birthday" for him, clapping happily, her eyes shining.

There was lots of positive energy in the room. It was a happy room; a room for love and laughter. Pavani could imagine herself in the room, growing old, with loved ones around her.

"I was upset to be ill on this day, of all days," said Raj. "I wanted to celebrate my birthday with you, and only you. Thank you for coming over, my dearest. I ought to have asked God for something more, I'm sure He would have given that too today!"

"I too wanted to spend the day with you today Raj. Your birthday is a special day for me. My life would have been meaningless without you."

Pavani spoke so earnestly, that Raj stopped short. With a pause, he said, "Pavani, I will always be with you. Always and forever! Wherever you go, I will be with you. I can't imagine my life without you. What you said is perfect. Life will be meaningless if you are not with me."

He moved closer to her, matching Pavani in earnestness, his heart thumping. Her heart raced like a trip-hammer. Raj was so close to her that he could not only hear her heartbeat but also feel the warmth of her breath.

Raj slowly put his hand to her waist and pulled her closer. Shyly, she lowered her eyes. Raj's lips were hardly an inch away from hers.

The air seemed charged and suddenly warm. They both knew what would come next and wanted to savour the delicious moments of anticipation. After a couple of minutes, Raj said, "May I ask for the most precious birthday gift?"

Pavani nodded and Raj kissed her. Breathless, she pulled away too soon. Raj held her face in his hands and claimed her lips again. This time she kissed him back. Raj was overwhelmed. She had given him the most perfect gift. Pavani's heart danced, her eyes turned starry. This was the most beautiful moment of her life!

Chapter - 12

When one thinks that everything is going as smooth as one could wish for, things change and a challenge crops up. Life never keeps one on a smooth ride for long. It throws in some turbulence every once in a while.

Pavani's life wasn't untouched either. Her life was smooth. She had the most loving parents and loving friends. She was doing well academically. To top it all, she had the love of someone who loved her more than anyone else in this universe. So, when everything was going so smooth, life had to throw a spanner into the works and mess everything up.

Jaya had not been feeling well. Though she had been complaining of back pain for the past few months, like a typical Indian woman, she was also too busy taking care of her family to find time to take care of herself.

Om was at Jabalpur for one week, to attend an official meeting. There was a big ordinance contract from the Indian Army after the Kargil war. The manufacturing was distributed amongst the defense manufacturing units. This meeting was to detail out what each unit will make. Since time was the essence, the timelines were also to be fixed. There was no scope for delay it even by a day as the security of the country was of paramount importance.

Almost every senior officer from each defense manufacturing unit was at Jabalpur for the meeting. Everyone had expected some free time but back-to-back strategic discussions and meetings kept everyone busy until late evening and back again early next morning to cover up two week's schedule in a week's time.

Within three days, everyone was exhausted and were looking forward to the meeting marathon to end when they were informed that the meeting would be extended by a week so everyone should inform to their families accordingly. DRDO, one of the establishments of Indian Defense, who designed new equipment for Indian Army, made some changes in design based on feedback received from Army and informed manufacturer that final blueprints would be delayed by couple of days so the training needed to be extended by another one week.

Everyone groaned. But the work was most critical and high-status assignment for the ordinance so no one could say anything. They had no choice but to call their families.

"Hello!" said Jaya.

"Hello Jaya! Om here!"

"Hello Om! How are you? How is your work going on?" she asked.

"I am fine," he said. "I'm stressed because the meetings go on for long hours. How are you? How is Pavani?"

"I am fine," she replied. "My backache is troubling me, that's all. Everything else is fine and so is Pavani. She has gone to meet Vaishali. Her exams preparation has started so she went to collect some notes."

"Okay! I hope you are taking care of yourself!" he said, concerned.

"Yeah, when are you coming back?"

"I... am coming back next week now. Our meeting has been extended till next week. I called to inform you. I am worried about your health. Tell Pavani to take you to the clinic. Do you want me to come? I can state extenuating circumstances and come," said Om.

"Oh no! You finish your work. I know how vital these meetings are. I don't want the whole thing to be derailed because of my silly back. I will manage fine. When you are back, we will go to the clinic. It is just a matter of another week.

"Pavani will be disappointed. She had planned a special dish this Sunday," she said.

"Oh, this is really a pity. I have to now wait for another one week for those special dishes. Ask Pavani to make those dishes at least for you. Why should you wait? Also, I insist you should go and get your checkup done. Don't aggravate the pain. I should have taken you to the clinic myself," he said.

"Okay, I will go with Pavani," said Jaya soothingly. "I am not sure if she will be able to spare the time from her exam preparations."

"I am sure she will find time. In any case, you must go!

"Okay, bye! You take care!"

"You too," Jaya said affectionately.

Jaya put the receiver back and sat down on the chair next to the phone. She was getting severe pain on back as was doing some work for quite some time.

It was not the first time, she was getting pain but she was keeping it to herself and not shared with anyone much about her health issues. Today it was severe and she was thinking that now she wouldn't keep it to herself and share it with family.

She tried to get up but pain was so severe and it restricted her to get up. She laid herself down on the chair. Her eyes were closed and full of tears as it was beyond her sufferance.

She kept herself for some more time in the same position. When she found that it was not getting better, she wasn't having any other choice but to call Pavani.

She slowly picked up the receiver and dialed Vaishali's number to call Pavani back home.

In next half an hour, Pavani was at home. For the first time, she saw her mother in so much pain. She could feel her pain and was cursing herself as she never persuaded her mother to take rest or insisted her to go to Doctor.

Pavani tried to help her mother to get up but she was in so much pain that her effort went in vain. The pain was continuously getting worse. When Pavani found no other option, she called Ordinance clinic for an ambulance.

In next few minutes, the ambulance was at their doorstep though they had shifted out of the Ordinance Township but being an employee, the medical team was quick to respond and helped them.

Supporting nurse staff, accompanying with ambulance, immediately picked Jaya up in the stretcher and rushed her to the hospital. Pavani was also with her mother and was unaware that her father was not coming this weekend and was trying to console her mother by saying that you would be fine, Mom and we would be back before Papa returned from Jabalpur.

At the hospital, Jaya was attended to by the duty doctor. The doctor administered a painkiller for quick relief. Once her pain had subsided, he sent her for a few medical tests. Pavani was asked to get Jaya admitted while the doctor got the tests done.

Pavani had not expected that her mother would be ill enough to need hospitalization. She tried to ask the doctor if he could run the test and let Jaya discharge since there was no one at home. But the doctor insisted on getting Jaya admitted. Pavani had no choice but to agree.

Pavani rushed to a PCO booth outside the hospital to call Raj and Vaishali both. Apart from them, she didn't know who else to call?

In fifteen minutes, Vaishali was in the hospital. Raj had informed Amit; they too were on their way. Vaishali was also carrying dinner for Pavani.

When she saw Vaishali, Pavani burst into tears. Vaishali consoled her and gave her courage. Meanwhile, Raj and Amit had also reached the hospital. The presence of her three friends was a huge support to Pavani.

That night was one of the longest nights in Pavani's life. She was unable to accept that her mother was sick enough to be admitted in the hospital. She was very worried and scared, praying for her quick recovery.

Only one person was allowed inside the ward at one time. The entire gang camped in the lobby of the hospital with one of them inside with Jaya in turns.

During the night, the doctor had given Jaya painkiller again to make sure that she had a peaceful night.

Pavani wondered if she ought to call her father. She didn't want to throw him into a panic. She knew how deeply Om loved Jaya. She also knew that the assignment on which his father was, an important one for national security so she didn't want to make any decision or call to her father in hurry.

After deliberation, she decided not to call him. He was coming home on Sunday anyhow. There was no point raising an alarm. She had good friends to support her. She conveyed her decision to her gang and everyone supported her.

In the morning, Baua brought tea and snacks for all. Pavani insisted on sending everyone home to rest. Baua stayed back with Pavani.

Around 9 am, all medical test reports were ready and also senior doctors were in the hospital.

A panel of doctors led by Doctor Singh had discussion to conclude but they couldn't find anything abnormal in the reports. Finally they agreed to refer super specialty hospital to get it thoroughly examined.

Though there were most of the facilities available but it was limited to specialty level and Jaya needed further diagnostic.

Doctor Singh called Pavani in his cabin. Pavani and Baua both walked into his cabin. When both entered into the room, he was busy studying the report and writing something on hospital letterhead. Baua was looking at various mementos kept on the backside rack of his chair and admiring while Pavani was getting restless as she wanted to know what had happened to her mother.

After completing his comments on letterhead, Doctor Singh looked at Pavani. He removed his spectacle and gently rubbed his eyes before talking to her.

Those few seconds were really very long for Pavani, she wanted to know that how was her mother, what happened to her, would she be alright or she had some bigger problem so on and so forth. She was just waiting for the doctor to say something to her.

"You are Jaya's daughter?" asked Dr. Singh.

Pavani nodded. "And this is a family friend," she said when Dr. Singh turned to Baua.

"When your father is coming back?" he asked Pavani. "We may need him for a discussion."

Filled with a sudden dread, Pavani said, "Papa will be back in a couple of days. May I know what is wrong with my Mom?" she asked in a small voice.

Dr. Singh didn't want to have the discussion with someone this young, but had no choice.

"We looked at all the reports and studied. We also had a discussion with our expert panel. Unfortunately, we could not reach to any conclusion for her severe condition. Though we are suspecting something but we are not sure about it."

He took a deep breath and continued, both Pavani and Baua were continuously staring at the doctor and trying to understand what he wanted to convey.

"We need to refer her to Super Specialty Hospital for further diagnosis. If your father is coming after a couple of days, what we can do, we can give her some medicines and painkillers so that she finds some relief. Once your father is back, you can take her to the Super Specialty Hospital for a thorough checkup. Though it is not so urgent but we should not wait for long. We can discharge her, you can take her back home and let her take rest. No work, only rest. Okay!"

Pavani was taken aback. She really wished her father were home. This was the second time in her life when she was desperate to have her father with her. She thought for a few seconds and then asked.

"Doctor, if it is urgent, I can take her to another hospital right now."

"I understand your anxiety but that is not needed. You can wait for a couple of days but not so long. You can take her home and make sure that she is taking sufficient rest. Please make sure that she does not tire herself out."

Pavani nodded and came out of the cabin. Baua also followed her. Both went to the discharge counter. Baua was carrying enough money to pay the dues to get Pavani's mother discharged.

In an hour or so, Jaya was back home, lying in bed. Pavani told her that she was alright but needed complete rest. She did not share her full conversation with the doctor.

Jaya was looked relieved. She was feeling helpless without Om at home. She didn't want to burden her young daughter. When she heard that everything was alright, she heaved a sigh of relief.

Baua had already left. Pavani was tired. She asked her mother if she wanted to have something to eat. When Jaya didn't show any interest, Pavani made tea for her and served it to her with some biscuits.

After having tea, Jaya took her medicine and slept. Pavani slept next to her mother.

In an hour or so, Pavani's sleep was disturbed by the doorbell. Her mother was still sleeping.

She walked to the door, while gathering her hair into a pony-tail. It was Vaishali's mother holding a lunchbox in her hand.

She hugged Pavani and gently patted her back. Pavani almost burst into tears. Pavani knew Baua must have shared the entire conversation with the doctor with his mother. That's why she had come now to provide emotional support.

"When will be your father back? Have you talked to him?" asked Vashali's mother.

"Papa told me that he will be back on Sunday," Pavani said. "I haven't informed him yet as I didn't want to disturb him."

Vaishali's mother nodded though she did not agree. "Why don't you inform him? No point delaying it. His support is of utmost important to your mother at this time."

Pavani nodded and said, "Yeah Aunty, you are right but I do not want to disturb him. Anyway, he can't do much and will be worried unnecessarily."

Just then, Pavani heard her mother calling her.

Both ladies stood up and moved to the bedroom. Jaya had just woken up. When she saw Vaishali's mother, she tried to get up but she couldn't. Vaishali's mother signaled her to take rest.

Pavani sat next to her mother while Vaishali's mother sat in a chair nearby. After sitting quietly for some time. Pavani enquired, "Mummy, have you got a call from Papa? What is his plan? He is coming back on Sunday, isn't he?"

"Your Papa called me yesterday," said Jaya. "His meeting has got extended. Now he will be back next Sunday."

Pavani looked at her mother in dismay.

"I know you are worried about me but I will be alright in the next few days," said Jaya reassuringly. "We don't need to inform your Papa. He will worry and it will disturb his focus as well. It is better to let him finish his work in peace. Distracting him now will delay the whole operation. And you know how vital an assignment he is on at present."

"I know," she continued with a deep breath, "it will be hard for both of us to manage but I am sure, my brave daughter will support me in my decision."

"But Mom, it is important that Papa should know about your health and the current worsening situation. You need his support. I need his support. I am not as strong as you are. I want him with us right now," Pavani protested.

Jaya tried to get up with the support of her hands but she couldn't. Now that the effect of painkillers was going down. It had been more than few hours since she took the last dose. She almost cried in pain. Her eyes were filled with tears of agony. She slumped back when she saw she couldn't get up.

There was a pin-drop silence in the room except for the whirring of the ceiling fan. Pavani was almost sure that she would not listen to her mother and inform her father. Earlier she was thinking that he was coming in next couple of days and there was no reason to panic. But one more week, that was too much and that too when the doctor advised her to be shown to a specialist on priority. Though she was positive that her mother would be fine in the next few days and be on her feet as usual, but she wanted her father around. He was Pavani's strength. With him around, she could battle with any challenge.

Her reverie was broken when her mother held her hand and stroked it lovingly. She wanted to convey that she had already taken the decision.

"My princess, I know you are worried about me. I know you want to take me to the specialist as soon as possible. I know, you feel vulnerable without your father. But you know how sincere and dedicated your father is towards his responsibilities. He is a true patriot. For him the country's needs are paramount. My princess can't be so greedy. She is the world's strongest daughter. She can't let her fears take control of her courage!"

Still stroking her hand affectionately, Jaya continued, "This is your test to check how strong your shoulders are, to see *h*ow you manage all your responsibilities efficiently!"

Pavani knew that she is fighting a lost battle. Her mother had already presented her case very strongly. Though she wanted to argue and win it, she decided to lose the battle instead of troubling her mother in her fragile state.

"Though I am not convinced with your arguments and I want to call Papa right now but I understand your feelings and point of view and I respect that," said Pavani. "I will support you. I will not call Papa right now. We both will manage for the next few days. I am sure, you will be fine before Papa comes back."

Jaya smiled. Looked like she won a big battle tactically without firing a bullet. Pavani and Vaishali's mother smiled back at her.

This how Indian mothers are. They know how to convince their kids, be it any situation. They know how to create the perfect blend of emotion and intelligence to best influence their children.

When Ms Roy Chaudhary stopped, her eyes were wet, her voice was shaking and she was almost on the verge of crying. It looked like she was very attached to Pavani. Her voice was filled with Pavani's pain. The deeper she was going into the story, the more her attachment to Pavani was visible.

Mrinalini opened her bag and pulled out a pack of wet tissue from her bag and offered it to her. Ms Roy Chaudhary took them gratefully and wiped away her tears.

Chapter - 13

After a silence of a few moments, Ms Roy Chaudhary picked up a water bottle and gulped some water hurriedly. She put the bottle back and continued.

The next few days were really very tiring. Pavani was playing many roles. She was nursing her mother, she was taking care of her house, and she was making sure to find out time to study as well.

In this toughest time of life, her friends Vaishali and Raj were her lifeline. Though Raj was not a frequent visitor to her house, he called Pavani regularly. These two were the biggest source of strength to her. Without them whatever she was able to manage, might not have been possible.

Finally, those difficult days were over and it was time for Om's arrival. Pavani was waiting for him anxiously. Her eagerness was similar to the way she waited for him every evening in her childhood.

It was the same eagerness now. She knew her father was a magician. The way he had always solved all challenges life threw his way, he would also solve this one as well.

When Om reached home, Pavani hugged him and began to cry in relief. Om had no idea what she had endured in his absence. He was taken aback at her welcome. He tried to console her and gently patted her head.

"What happened to my princess?" he asked. "Why are you so sad? You know your Papa is a magician and will make everything alright. Tell me, what's the problem?"

She wiped her tears on her sleeve and smiled tremulously. Her father was home! Now he would make everything right!

She took Om's hand and took him to the bedroom. He found Jaya lying down. He knew Jaya wasn't the kind to lie down unless she was really sick. He recalled his last discussion with her and realized her backache must have got aggravated. He had no idea her pain was so severe!

He sat down beside Jaya and held her hand.

"Why did you two super-women not tell me what was going on here?"

Pavani wanted to say something, but Jaya stopped her. Her pain was still severe. It threatened to flow out her eyes in the form of tears.

"We didn't want to disturb you. Moreover, it is a small issue. It will get over now as you are back," declared Jaya bravely.

Om hugged them both, overwhelmed at the courage of his wife and daughter.

Chapter - 14

For the next few days, Jaya had a couple of appointments in a super speciality hospital. Post initial checkups, she was attended by an Oncologist because her reports indicated a malignancy. A biopsy later, it was confirmed. She had cancer of the uterus!

Keeping them from dwelling too long on this devastating news, the doctor immediately planned her treatment. The cancer had spread outside the uterus so it couldn't be removed. He put her on radiation immediately with chemotherapy to follow. It was a very costly and painful procedure but that was the last resort to get her healed.

Pavani was unable to comprehend how to deal with it. Just a few days back, she started building her dreams where she had someone else apart from her family and within a few days, she was required to accept one of the hardest truths of the life-that nothing was permanent.

Just when things were shaping up for her, came this blow to shatter all her dreams. She wanted to share her happy news with her parents, but this was hardly the time.

Om was also having a very tough time to accept the truth. Though he was very strong and always open to accept the realities, this came as a nightmare to him too.

Pavani was praying every moment for things to normalize. She planned to start her preparations for CAT post her annual exam but now she was facing the biggest exam of the life.

Pavani's exams were around the corner. She had added responsibilities to manage now. During the day, she managed the household and took care of her mother. At night, exhausted by the demands of the day, she focused on her exam preparations. When her father took her mother for Chemotherapy, she had some additional time to connect with Raj and Vaishali.

She used to wonder how her mother managed everything at home, now she had to manage not only the home but also her studies. Surprisingly, she was handling everything well. Reservoirs of courage and hardihood, she never suspected she had, now came to the fore. She became more calm and stable than she had ever been in her carefree days.

When we take things for granted, God is compelled to create a wake-up call. He reminds us not to become complacent. When life throws a challenge at you, you must deal with it to the best of your ability. Pavani was doing exactly that. She was making sure that she has no cause for regret. She never wanted to feel later that she could have done bit more.

Both Vaishali and Raj were very concerned for her but they had no idea how to help her. They shared their notes and tips to make her exam preparations easier. But they could not help with her household duties to a very large extent. They knew she needed emotional support more than anything else and for that, they were always available.

Om had taken Jaya for Chemotherapy when Raj dropped by. Pavani was thrilled to see him.

"Pavani, how is Aunty now?" he asked.

"She is fine now. I-I-I think she is fighting the disease well," Pavani said.

Raj rubbed his hands, a little embarrassed. It was really hard to know the right thing to say in such situations.

"How is your exam's preparation going on?" he asked.

"I am trying to find the time. Honestly, it is really hard. I am still not able to accept that such a thing has happened with my Mom. The thought distracts me!" said she.

She started crying. Raj took her in his arms and put her head on his chest, stroking it gently as she let her fears out.

"Don't cry my angel, you are a brave girl," Raj said, his voice low. "I know you will win through this. You are immensely strong and determined. I never saw anyone like you who has such tenacity. I am sure, this turbulent time will soon be over!"

Pavani was still crying. She knew that the coming few months would be very tough. She wanted to discuss something with Raj since he was a part of her future. She wiped her tears away and composed herself. She sat down and asked Raj to sit too.

"Raj, I want to talk to you about something. Since you are the one with whom I am planning my entire life, I must tell you what I have been thinking of doing. I don't want to take any decision in haste and without discussing with you. I hope, you will support me."

Raj nodded and she continued.

"Raj, with mom so unwell, her treatment may continue for many months. My father and mother need me at present. I want to switch to part-time stream for the final year. I can't afford to go to college for classes every day and if there is less attendance, they may not allow me to sit in the final exam. It would be better to switch gears right now so that I don't need to worry about my attendance. I really wanted to continue with regular college but that seems unrealistic at present. I am sure when I talk to Papa, he will not agree to it. But I will convince him if you support me."

Raj was surprised. This is the last thing he expected her to say. But he trusted her judgement. He controlled himself and said, "Pavani, I will support every decision you take. You must have thought through this and weighed all the pros and cons. This may disturb your life. Your dreams may shatter if things don't go the way you are planning. We have many plans for our future. I hope, you have analyzed the impact of this decision! Also, I am sad that I wouldn't be able to see you in college every day!"

Pavani nodded. Raj gave her a thumbs-up and hugged her. Pavani was greatly relieved that day. Obtaining Raj's support was vital for her. Tears of relief ran into the fabric of Raj's shirt.

Chapter - 15

Pavani's exams were over, so she had more time to take care of her mother. Her treatment was still going on. Life was getting into a normal routine as Om, Jaya and Pavani everyone accepted the truth and their destiny.

Raj and Vaishali were regular visitors. Sometimes she also went to meet them.

One day she was in the kitchen and preparing tea for her parents. Om and Jaya were sitting in the drawing room. When Jaya was sure that Pavani is not around, she asked Om, "I wanted to talk to you about something. I hope you understand and hear me out."

Om nodded and Jaya continued.

"Whenever I sleep and think about my life, I always think that my life is not too long and I need to do a lot before I die. Though you and Pavani are taking care of me, one responsibility keeps me awake all night. I want to see Pavani get married before I go. I don't know how many days I still have."

Om tried to say something but Jaya stopped him.

"Please don't say, no. I want to see her as a bride before I die. Will you not fulfil my last wish?"

Before Om could react, Pavani, who was just entering the drawing room with tea in her hand, intervened. She knew what was going on in her mother's mind. She kept the tray on the table and sat next to her mother. She held her hands and said, "Mom, I know you are worried about Papa and me. I know you want to see me married. But why do you think you won't be with us? You will be with us not for few days or months but for many years!"

Pavani's eyes were wet and Jaya's tender touch was making her emotionally weak. Jaya's eyes were also wet. Before a teardrop could escape her eyes, Pavani wiped it quickly and continued.

"Mom, I am sure, you will be alright in the next few months. Post that, we will have a mega party. After that whatever you want to plan, you can do so. And... and I am sure you can plan it in a better way and we all will support it."

Jaya looked at Pavani in wonder. Pavani was so motherly, taking care of her as young mothers deal with their toddlers. Pavani was convincing her mother about something she herself was unsure of. Time stood still for the family. Like all families, they had many dreams. But their cruel circumstances had swept all their dreams away, leaving just one-that of Jaya's total recovery.

Jaya hugged Pavani and Om hugged them both. They remained bound for many moments, each hiding moist eyes from the other two. None of them were worried about themselves. Their tears were coz of the stress and suffering of the other two.

The emotional moment left each of them strengthened. They separated with just one fervent wish in their hearts-that everything would be normal very soon.

Pavani gave the tea to her parents and took hers.

"Papa," she began. "I want to say something. Hope you will give me a patient hearing."

Om looked at her and said, "Looks like today is the day for me to give a patient hearing to both of you. First your Mom and now to you. Okay, tell me. What's going on in your mind?"

"Papa, I know, last few days were very tough for all of us. Mom is going through the worst of it. We can only support her mentally, physically and emotionally. It was not easy for me to take this decision but I feel this is the best for all of us."

Om and Jaya were listening to her wondering when their innocent, carefree girl turned into a responsible and sensible human being. They didn't know what was going on in her mind but certainly sounded very serious and mature.

Pavani took a deep breath and continued.

"When we found about mom's illness, for a few days I wondered why this calamity had fallen upon us. What wrong had we done? Perhaps God only gives troubles to the people who can bear them. Maybe challenges are sent to make us stronger. They do say adversity is a character builder. Time will reveal the reason to us I am sure.

"The last few days were tough on us all. Mom's treatment will continue for another four-five months. After thinking things through, I have decided that I will continue my studies part-time instead of attending college full-time. That way I need not worry about my attendance. I can look after everything as well as keep studying. I know both of you will not like it but we need to be practical. I am sure you will also agree that my decision is the right thing to do at this time."

"My little princess," said Om, visibly moved. "I know, things are not in our favour but taking such a hard decision without first consulting with us is not fair. You should think again. This is not a small decision, you are putting your entire life, your dreams, and your career at stake. You wanted to pursue management studies, how will you fulfil your dream? This is a short-term challenge. We will keep some full-time help to manage. I am sure, your mom will be alright in a short while. She can also supervise the help. I think you should not be so firm on your decision. You should rethink it."

Jaya also nodded.

"Papa, my decision is firm," said Pavani. "Also, I am not sacrificing anything. I will continue preparing for CAT, I know it is hard but I will give it my best. I know, next one year is going to pretty tough but I know I can manage it fine. I just need you to say yes!"

Om hugged her and murmured, "When did my angel grow up?"

For the next three-four months, Jaya's chemotherapy continued and she made great progress. She was now getting better. Pavani was managing her responsibilities pretty well. She took admission for completing her final year part-time. She also joined correspondence program to prepare for CAT exam. She kept the ball rolling.

Raj was very helpful. He was always there to help whenever Pavani needed. Raj and Pavani both attempted the CAT exam and continued their final year graduation study.

Jaya's treatment was over and now she had no sign of pain. Her health was much better now. She began taking care of a few things around the house. That eased Pavani's responsibilities to some extent. The doctor had put her on medication and recommended regular checkups.

The CAT results were out. Raj had cleared the exam but she hadn't. Looked like her multi-responsibility did distract her. She was happy for Raj but extremely disappointed for herself.

Pavani called Raj and congratulated him. Raj knew that it was hard for Pavani to accept that she couldn't make her dream come true. To him, she was a winner because she had won the race of life. He tried to convince her that she had done very well. Juggling so many balls is no easy task. She had passed the most important test of her life with flying colours.

Pavani was aware of what she had accomplished. She still wished she had not lost the opportunity to clear CAT as well.

Raj got selected for IIM Bangalore after an interview and focus group discussion. It was a piece of great news for everyone. Now everyone was focusing on their final year graduation exam results.

Everyone had done well in final exams but Pavani stole the show with her marks. She scored better marks than her entire gang. She was clearly sharper in her entire gang. Thrilled to the core, she decided to attempt the CAT exam again next year.

Raj packed his bags and headed to Bangalore. He was now ready to add another chapter of his life far from his earlier life where he would get new friends, new ideas and new lessons for life.

Chapter - 16

Raj and Pavani were constantly in touch on the phone. It was a major change for Raj. He was coping with many things at the same time. Often he stayed up long into the night. Things were not easy. Away from the comforts of home, in a new environment, everything contributed in making the transition an uphill task.

Raj was trying his level best to cope with the cultural shock that a lad of Kanpur would naturally experience in the cosmopolitan culture of Bangalore. His heavy academic load was also a challenge for him. He was looking at things in a completely different way.

He called Pavani often. Her encouragement held him together and gave him renewed motivation to face his challenges. Pavani's words helped him immensely. Weeks dissolved into months. Finally, Raj reached a level of confidence where he was able to declare to Pavani that he was sure he would not only survive in the new place but thrive. He also told her that without her, he would have returned to Kanpur, defeated.

Jaya wanted to get Pavani married as soon as possible. She knew she was living on borrowed time which may be with drawn any moment. She insisted that Om begin a matrimonial search for Pavani. Pavani wanted one more chance to try for CAT along with her post-graduation but Jaya was firm on her decision.

Pavani knew if she didn't tell her parents about Raj, she would regret it all her life. One evening she told her parents everything.

Since Raj was known to the family, neither Jaya nor Om had a problem. Om was happy that his daughter had chosen the best man by herself.

Raj planned to visit Kanpur for Diwali. Pavani thought it would be the right occasion to approach Raj's family too. Raj agreed and assured her that he would talk to her parents once he was there.

When Raj reached Kanpur, he told his mother, Janaki, about Pavani. Janaki was a very simple lady. A charming, always smiling and very God fearing. Her life revolved around Raj and his father.

Though she liked Pavani, she wasn't sure how Raj's father Ram Lal would react. Ram Lal was a businessman and perspective was always that of profit.

He had always referred to Raj as a blank cheque when he discussed him with anyone. Janaki knew his mercenary side very well, hence was sceptical.

Though she was unsure, Janaki assured Raj that she would talk to Ram Lal and convince him. Raj was elated and shared the great news with Pavani. She told her parents and Om decided to visit Raj's house.

On the day after Diwali, Om visited Ram Lal. He was carrying a box of sweets, a typical Indian tradition of not visiting anyone's house empty-handed, especially when going for an important discussion.

Raj introduced him to his parents. Ram Lal greeted Om and gave him a warm welcome. While Raj was excited, his mother Janaki was nervous. She hadn't got a chance to discuss the issue with her husband. Knowing him, she was not sure how would he react.

She took the tea and some snacks to the drawing room. While Raj served Om with tea, Janaki tried to call Ram Lal aside but he missed her signal.

Ram Lal enquired about Jaya. Though he was making polite conversation, he was surprised at Om's unexpected visit.

Om was surprised in turn. He was under the impression that the purpose of his visit would be clear to Ram Lal.

"Ram Lal Ji," he said at last, "you know Pavani very well and have met with her many at times in the past. You also know that Jaya is not keeping well. She wants to get her married as soon as possible. We thought we could wait until Pavani completes her post-graduation but Jaya's insistence has compelled me to look for a suitable groom for Pavani immediately. The wedding can be held after a while but at least let us fix the marriage so that she feels relieved."

Ram Lal nodded. "That's a great thought, I think," he said. "You should look for a suitable match and go ahead with her marriage. Have you found someone? Do you have anyone in your mind?"

Now Om was certain that Ram Lal was unaware of the Raj and Pavani's relationship. He was in a dilemma whether to continue or come back again some other day. With Om, pensive, the room fell silent. The silence was broken by Janaki.

"Listen, I need you to take something down from the loft. I need it urgently. Please come inside and do it now."

"Please excuse me *bhaisahab*. I'll come right back!"

Ram Lal glared at her. He couldn't refuse her though and followed her inside the house, seething. In brief, Janaki told him about Raj and Pavani. Ram Lal came out to the drawing room again.

His face was red with anger. Staring balefully at Om, he sat down.

"So you are here for Raj," he said. "I wasn't aware of it. I didn't know that Raj and Pavani like each other. Before we talk any further, there are a few things I would like to clarify so that there are no confusions."

He looked at Om who was looking now anxious so he continued.

"I have many expectations of Raj. That's the reason I planned for his management course almost from his childhood. We sacrificed our desires to save for his education. He is the biggest investment in my own future. I have a more than a few expectations from his marriage. I hope you understand what I mean."

He took a deep breath and continued.

"Firstly, I don't think we can proceed with the wedding right now. He has just completed a few months of his course. The wedding can only happen after he gets into a job. Secondly, I was looking for marriage within our caste but if I am going out of the caste, I need to have some reason to justify it to all my family members, society and friends. You understand, right?"

Om's fingers were entwined. A thick cord formed in his neck but he listened in stony silence.

"Lastly, I had decided on a dowry of twenty lacs for his marriage if I get him married to someone within my caste. Since you do not belong to my caste, I think thirty lacs sounds reasonable for his marriage. We can discuss on dates, cash or kind subsequently."

Om was completely shocked. His face had paled with the effort of controlling his temper. He had come to visit his daughter's future family, not a cold-blooded trader! Ram Lal was trading the happiness of his son, his future and his life! And at such an impossible price! Om took a deep breath and made his decision.

"Thank you, Ram Lal Ji! I came here on the insistence of my daughter. I have heard you out. I am a pretty well off and Pavani is my only child. I will not send my daughter off empty-handed. I have also planned many things for her. I would like to not just fulfil her dreams but also ours. But...But..."

Om fumbled and took a deep breath. Ram Lal was still looking at him. Om continued.

"I do not think we can really meet an expectation as high as yours. I was here to make my daughter happy. I have fulfilled all her wishes from the time she was a child. This time, however, she has asked for something which is beyond the financial status of her father."

He took another deep breath and continued.

"I am sure when I tell her what happened here she will understand why I returned empty-handed. She is a very mature and sensible girl. I am immensely proud of her!"

With that, Om stood up and walked out of Raj's house. Ram Lal and Janaki were left staring in surprise, not sure how to react.

Om told Jaya and Pavani everything that had happened. Raj had told Pavani that his father was money-minded but she had no idea he would put a price on his own son's happiness.

The challenges of the past six months had made Pavani very strong. She didn't break-down. She was proud of her father for refusing to the unreasonable demand. She was happy her father did not give way to emotion though she knew how deeply he loved her.

Raj called a couple of times but Pavani didn't talk to him. He was leaving the next day. He called Vaishali to bring Pavani to the railway station as he wanted to talk to her before leaving for Bangalore.

Vaishali too wanted to give her friends the chance to clear up the confusions between them. Making an excuse for why she needed to go to the railway station, Vaishali took Pavani there. Once they reached the station, they met Raj and Amit. As soon as she saw Raj, Pavani understood why Vaishali had brought her. She was furious with Vaishali and told her so.

Amit and Vaishali went off with another excuse, leaving the two lovers together. Raj asked Pavani to sit on a bench and sat next to her himself.

"Pavani, I am so sorry for whatever has happened that day at home!"

Pavani didn't say anything. Raj tried to hold her hand but Pavani jerked his hand away. He knew why she was upset. Again he tried to hold her hand. This time she let him.

After a silence of a few moments, Raj said, "Pavani, I am so sorry. Whatever has happened, it should have not happened but nothing was in my hand. I discussed with Mom but because of Diwali preparation, she did not get the time to discuss it with Papa."

Pavani was hearing it patiently without reacting as she wanted to hear his side of the story as well.

"You know very well that my Papa is a bit traditional and was shocked when he heard about us. Please understand and support me instead of being so hard just because of one incident. I need more time to convince him, challenge his orthodox mindset and bring him to our side."

When Pavani still didn't react, Raj continued.

"Do you know how much I love you Pavani? I can't go to Bangalore knowing you are angry. I want to sort this matter out but unfortunately, I can't do much about it right now. We need to wait for some more time to convince everyone. We can't start our new life when we know our parents are unhappy."

Pavani cooled down when Raj said that.

"Raj, tell me one thing, if things don't work out in our favour, will you still stand by me and marry me?"

Raj nodded. That nod was all Pavani needed. She was assured that Raj would always be with her. Her heart soared with joy and her eyes shone!

"Raj, whether we are happy or sad, whether it is rain, summer or cold, if you are with me, we can fight any battle. Raj, please always be with me. I will break completely if you are not with me. You don't know what I went through during the past few days! Please don't put me through that torture again!"

She burst into tears. Raj held her close and let her cry, his own eyes moist. He promised himself that he would never let her down, no matter what.

He knew he would need to find a way to convince his father, but he was determined to never let go of this trusting girl!

Chapter - 17

Once Raj reached Bangalore, he kept in touch with Pavani regularly. Pavani was assured that she had a great understanding with Raj and he would stand by her.

Raj's third semester was around the corner. Pavani suggested limiting her daily calls to a single weekly call. One day, Pavani called Raj mid-week. He was surprised. They had agreed to talk only on Sundays.

"Hello!" he said.

"Hello Raj!" she responded. Raj could hear the pain in her voice. He was alarmed.

"What has happened? Why do you sound so stressed? Is everything alright?" he asked.

When she heard the love in Raj's voice, she burst into tears. A girl who had not shown a trace of sadness to her parents in the past few months, sounded like she had lost a long battle.

Raj tried to console her and finally, after few minutes, she controlled herself.

"Are you okay now?" Raj asked. "Can you please let me know what has happened? Why are you crying?"

There was complete silence from her so Raj asked again, this time coaxingly.

"Pavani, if you don't share your pain with me, how will I know? Tell me! I can't bear to see you crying like this. You are a brave girl. I derive strength from you. It is because of you that I am still here. If you cry like this, what will happen to me? Tell me what has happened!"

After a few seconds of silence, he heard her voice again.

"Raj, I have some bad news. Mom's quarterly investigation reports are not good. The doctor has asked us to go for some more tests. If those reports are also not good, we have to go for a biopsy again as they are suspecting reoccurrence of cancer."

"Oh my God! That's too bad!" Raj exclaimed. He took a deep breath and continued, "You don't worry, things will be alright. I am sure that the next report will be alright."

Pavani knew that Raj was just trying to console her.

That day she realised the uncertainty of life. Things can change any moment and go haywire. They don't always go the way you want them to. Life was one long rollercoaster. She knew Raj would always be with her but in her present state, she could trust in nothing.

"Raj, may I ask you a question? I hope, you will answer it honestly."

"You know I will Pavani," said Raj.

"I know, your father has his own ideas about our marriage. Those values are important to him. I don't say that he is wrong but that's the way he is and we have to accept him with his viewpoint. But if he does not change his mind, it will be impossible for us to get married. If that is so, what would be your decision? Would you be with him or you would stand by me?"

"Why are you asking this question right now?" asked Raj, a little rattled. "I told you earlier as well, I will talk to them when the right time comes. I am sure he will listen to me."

"I know I should not ask this question. But I no longer know what to trust. Anything that I lean on seems to be giving way under me. Everything was so wonderful until a couple of years ago but suddenly everything had turned topsy-turvy. Things were getting settled between us. I was expecting good times ahead but I got another jolt. I have low hope from life now. I just need to know if I can lean on you," she murmured sadly.

It was hard for Raj to say with conviction that things would work in their favour. If they do not, he would go ahead with marriage without taking consent of his family. Nor could he share his doubts with Pavani knowing she was running low on confidence. There was a war going in his mind and finally, he thought to be pragmatic in his approach. He took a deep breath and said, "Pavani, I really don't think you should worry about it. I am sure I'll get a good job after completing my studies. I will make all efforts to convince him and get him to agree."

He paused while Pavani eagerly waited to hear more. His words would determine her future, she knew that. The pause stretched on heavily, as long to her as the passing of days, not moments.

"Pavani, if my father doesn't agree to it, I will go ahead and marry you without his consent. Though that is something which neither you nor I want. However, if that is our destiny, we will get married without his blessings. I am sure, he would be angry with us but he can't remain so forever!"

Finally, Pavani heard what she was waiting impatiently for. His words gave her courage and induced a positive surge of happiness in her. She had something to look forward to and a reason to be cheerful.

She didn't know what the future held. Would things work in her favour? Would life go as she and Raj were planning? Would her mother be with her?

Whatever the doubts and uncertainties, one thing she knew. Things may fall apart but in the end, her life would be beautiful and exciting.

* * *

Raj's exams were over and he was back at Kanpur for a short break before the new semester began. Pavani was struggling. She was not able to cope with the challenges at home. With cancer having recurred, the stress on the family was much heavier. The treatment was much more intensive and expensive. The treatment cost had exceeded the insurance coverage and Om had to dig into his savings. Then came the time when he even had to dip into the funds he had set aside for Pavani's marriage.

Like any other father, Om had dreamt of marrying Pavani off with pomp and grandeur. But destiny had other plans. Their rollercoaster life was telling him that life doesn't go the way you plan. It was not a straight line but full of peaks and valleys like a heartbeat. Perhaps these ups and downs are what keep us alive. A straight line is not representative of life. Perhaps this is why our lives are unpredictable. The rollercoaster they were on, made Pavani so tense that her studies took a back seat and her topmost priority was to look after her mother and to take care of her family.

Raj met Pavani a few times. He was meeting a girl who was worried about her family and her heart and soul were with them. Each meeting was emotional. Raj was missing his erstwhile Pavani. The chuckling, mischievous Pavani who had many plans for her life, was gone. Today's Pavani was an anxious, frightened, distressed, trembling, nervous girl who had lost all hope.

Chapter - 18

In December Raj called Pavani to tell her that he had been selected to one of the MNCs and would be joining their Mumbai office. Pavani was thrilled. His success and achievements were linked not only to his future but also to her own. There was no doubt in her mind that their futures were entwined.

Raj asked her about her mother's health. Her answer gave him little hope. He knew Pavani was going through the toughest time of her life and was at the verge of collapse. She needed his support. It was his turn to stand by her as she had stood by him. His success was not his alone. Her support and encouragement had brought him to where he was today, he could not deny it.

After a long silence, Raj asked her, "How are you managing everything? How is Uncle?"

Pavani was quiet. It was a happy day for him, for her. She didn't want to ruin his day. She wanted him to enjoy the day like never before without really worrying about her so she just whispered, "Everything is fine Raj. Papa is also okay."

After that, she fell silent. Raj could hear the pain in her voice. He tried to console her and said, "Pavani, don't worry, everything will be alright. You are my brave *bachcha* who gives me courage and positivity. You cannot be disheartened. No matter how dark night is, it will end eventually. There will be a glorious morning after the dark night; certainty after uncertainty and glee after gloom. One needs to keep hope alive. That's the way life runs. If we don't have the uncertainties, we might stop being grateful to the Almighty for what He has given us!"

Raj took a deep breath and paused. He was not sure if there was any impact on Pavani. "Are you there, Pavani?" he asked.

"Yes, I am," she murmured. She was silent for a long while. "You have now become a true management person. I know, things will become good soon."

With a deep-drawn sigh, she said, "Raj, I need to now know when you are going to talk to your parents about us. Mom wants to get me married soon. We were waiting for you to get a job so that you could have a candid discussion with your parents and we can really convince them about our future."

This was something which always made Raj uncomfortable. He knew that the discussion was not so easy to take up with his father. Though his mother was in his favour but convincing his father was also necessary. Pavani's family had no problem with the match so there was not much required at her end but Raj needed to subdue a potential volcano.

There was a long silence over the phone. Now it was Pavani who enquired, "Are you there, Raj?"

"Yes, I am there. I was just thinking how to tackle this. I need to talk to my father if my mother is unable to talk to him," he said.

"Yeah, I think, you should talk to him," she said.

"Let's do one thing. I will talk to you next week after discussing with them. I am not sure how successful I will be but at least let me initiate the discussion and try to convince him," Raj said.

Raj's hesitant, doubtful tone worried Pavani. Yet the fact that he was willing to take the bull by the horns gave her a little courage.

The next few days were tough for Pavani. The suspense was killing her. She argued with herself this way and that. Would Raj's father agree? How would Raj convince him? Would her dream to have a happily married life with Raj be in reality or would it just remain a pipe dream?

When there was no call from Raj for almost ten days. Pavani tried to call him. Raj didn't take her calls. Every unanswered call stretched her anxiety higher. She promised herself, she wouldn't call and wait for him to call but each time she lost her patience and called him, only to be plunged in deeper despair.

Finally, after fifteen days, she got a call from Raj. At first, she thought of ignoring the call but her desperation stopped her. She had no stomach to play games.

"Hi Raj!" she said, trying to sound composed.

"Hi, Pavani! How are you?" said Raj hesitantly.

"How do you think, I should be?" shot Pavani, her relief goading her into a reaction.

Raj got an answer he hadn't expected though he knew that the conversation he was to have with Pavani would be the most difficult conversation he had ever had in his life.

"Hmmm, I know! I saw your calls but..." Raj's voice petered off.

Pavani was silent. After a few moments of silence, Raj asked, "Hmmm! So you want to know what the outcome of my discussion with my father is?"

"Umm, well... Yes, I do," Pavani replied, her heart filled with foreboding.

"Pavani, you know, how much I love you and I want to live my rest of the life with you."

He took a pause and continued

"But at the same time, I am also mindful that we should have a life with our families together not just our own tiny world as the birds do."

Pavani was all ears. Her fingers were fidgeting nervously.

"Pavani, don't get me wrong. I-I-I am sure you will also agree that we want to make our life together only with the blessings of elders."

Pavani nodded though he couldn't see her nod.

"I had many discussions with my father in the past couple of weeks but I haven't got his consent till now. I tried all my ways to convince him but he is unmovable. I know him, he is a bit stubborn in his decision. He is like a coconut-hard on the outside but pretty soft inside. I am sure, in the next few days I will be able to get him to our side."

Pavani was shocked. She couldn't understand how Raj would get his father to agree when he hadn't been able to do in two weeks.

Would her life keep dragging like this? Would she never get any happiness in her life? She was feeling helpless and was angry with God. Why had He made her a girl? Why not a boy? Why could Raj's father be like her's who was so fair and reasonable? Would life keep throwing her off a cliff like this? Did she have to accept this or did she have any other choice in life?

There was a storm of questions in her mind and she had no answers to any of them. She wanted a straight answer from her life. She was now tired of the ups and downs in every area of her life. Involuntarily, she bunched up her fist. Her jaws were clamped together. She had never known herself to be as angry as she was in that moment.

She took a deep breath and took a decision.

"Raj, our paths are different from now on. I do not see any reason for us to be together. I can't live under the sword for the rest of my life."

Raj knew the conversation would be difficult but this was the last thing he expected. It was checkmate for him. He was thinking that she would agree to give him some more time but she was absolutely firm on her decision.

He had no idea how to handle a situation which was going out of his hand. He tried to control himself.

"What do you think, Pavani?" he asked, trying to sound masterful. "You think I am not worried? Am I not concerned about our dreams, our life together? I am also as concerned as you are but we need to be a little patient. Don't you agree?"

"I know, Raj! And I-I was pretty hopeful about our relationship. That's the reason I gave you enough time to get your father's consent," she said, her voice broken. "Y-Y-You know, Raj, we have given more than a year for this situation to get resolved but it seems to be getting more and more tangled. Your father is adamant and you are not able to convince him. How do you think you would come out of this situation?"

"I know it is hard but we should give some time to it. I know a year is a good enough time but maybe a little bit more. Maybe another few days."

Raj thought it would give him sufficient time to get Pavani calm down and he would find some solution.

"No. We don't have too much time. My mother's health is deteriorating day by day. It seems she is living only to see me get married. Her borrowed time is running out."

"We need to get some decision now or maximum in the next one week."

Raj knew he had to take a stand, one way or the other. "Okay Pavani," he said. "You are right, we have to take some decision. We can't keep delaying it to eternity. Give me one week's time and ask Uncle to go and meet my father next Sunday. I will make sure that I convince him before that. He loves me a lot. I will go all out this time. This time I will be emotional, not practical."

Pavani was a little surprised. She was not sure that her firm decision would draw such a commitment from Raj. She was happy. It was good for both of them. A feeble ray of hope lit up her tired eyes once more.

"Are you sure or you need more time?" Pavani asked.

"Yes, I am sure. You tell Uncle to have some free time to visit my father next Sunday and this time he will have a positive outcome!" Raj sounded confident.

Pavani was elated. She thanked God silently. Her eyes filled up and her tears spilt over. She was too happy to stop them.

"Love you, Raj!" she whispered.

"Love you too," responded Raj.

Chapter - 19

Om had just returned after meeting with Raj's father.

He looked upset and disturbed. When he'd gone to meet Raj's father at Pavani's insistence, he was pretty sure that Raj would support him. But Raj kept completely silent when his father was bargaining hard and demanding what he wanted.

Raj's father was not willing to budge from his demand. Raj did chime in once or twice but he was neither firm nor effective in countering his father's arguments. Ram Lal had categorically declared that he would not agree for anything less than the amount he had spoken of earlier. Anyone who wanted to get their daughter to marry to his son had to be willing to compensate him for the money he had invested in his son.

Raj was pushing his mother to convince his father but she too was ineffective. Finally, Raj left it to his father to convey his final decision to Om.

Om knew that Raj was the best groom for his daughter. Moreover, he knew how much Pavani love Raj. The dowry being demanded was really too high. He had some money saved for Pavani's marriage but a large chunk of it had been spent on Jaya's treatment. That had made a big hole in his savings. He was also not sure how much more would be needed for Jaya's treatment. He could not commit to something he wasn't sure he would be able to honour.

Pavani understood that things had not gone well, from the heaviness with which Om threw himself down on the sofa. Pavani offered him water. He requested her to make tea for him.

Though she was in the kitchen, her ears were tuned to the drawing room. She was sure the news wasn't great but she needed to know how bad it was. It was extremely important to her.

Putting the water to boil, she crept close to the drawing room noiselessly. She put her ears to the wall to hear what her father was talking about.

Om was sitting with his eyes closed, head resting on the back of the sofa. He didn't know where he should start from. Before he could say anything, Jaya broke the silence.

"What happened?" she asked. "Why are you so upset? Was your discussion with Raj's father not fruitful? Are they still not budging from their demand?"

Before Om replied, he glanced towards the kitchen door to ensure the Pavani wasn't in earshot.

"Jaya, I was thinking that things will work out as Pavani was sure that Raj will support her and value their relationship. I know she trusts Raj absolutely. His father's demand remains the same. He refused to come down even by a single rupee. Raj tried to convince him but I do not think he has any say at home. His father was very firm. Raj was just silent. When I looked at him, he lowered his eyes, looking embarrassed and ashamed. I understood that the battle was already lost."

He took a deep breath and continued.

"I had planned a grand wedding for Pavani. In the last couple of years, our medical expenses were too high. I don't have an arrangement of more than ten lacs now. I am not sure how long that will last, given our medical expenses ahead."

Om sounded like a defeated father who had lost all hopes of fulfilling his daughter's dreams. He had planned many things for his angel. He wanted to give her the world. Today, a social evil had defeated him. He had no support from society to help him out of the situation. There was no one to appeal to, no one to intervene. He had never felt so helpless in his life. He could see things were fizzling out but he could do nothing except watching happening it helplessly.

Jaya broke into loud wails. She was cursing herself as if everything had happened because of her. Om looked at her and asked, "What happened? Why are you crying?"

"This has happened because of me. If I had died instead of draining off our savings in medical treatments, at least you would have had sufficient money to settle Pavani with someone she loves. I am the cause of her shattered dreams."

Om tried to soothe her but Jaya was inconsolable. The pain of her illness had already weakened her severely. Her remaining courage broke too with this final jolt. She began to weep and beat her chest. When nothing worked, Om tried to tell her to keep quiet in case Pavani overhears her. Jaya was too broken to heed his whispered advice. She blamed herself for causing misery in her daughter's life.

Of course, Pavani had heard everything. She ran to her room and banged the door shut.

When Om heard the sound of the door closing, he realised that Pavani heard everything. He tried to leave Jaya but she held his hand very tightly. He called out to Pavani from the drawing room but she didn't reply.

Om took Jaya to her room and asked her to relax. Jaya continued to cry bitterly. Om went quickly to check on Pavani. Her door was closed. He banged on it, called out to her coaxingly and asked her to open the door. There was no answer. He could hear that she was crying but he couldn't do much. He rushed back to Jaya.

Jaya was lying on her bed keeping her face on the pillow. Om offered her water. Jaya took a couple of sips with great difficulty and lay down again, sobbing afresh.

Pavani looked at the fan and got up. Jaya's words rang in her ears. She, who had been courageous all these months, was broken. The thought of Jaya blaming herself, wishing herself dead! Oh, the horror of it! All because a greedy man wouldn't let go of his avarice. It was better she ceased to exist! Filled with a wild determination, she picked a pen and paper from her table and started writing.

'Dear Mom and Papa,

I know you wanted to give your best to me. My life seems to be a total disaster. I love you both more than my life! Mom, I can't bear the thought of you feeling guilty for the money that was spent on your treatment. You didn't ask for the disease! I have seen you suffer under it... and now to hear you say this has just broken me.

Before more chaos blights our lives, I will end this worthless life to give both of you some relief.

Please forgive me. I know I am letting you down. But this is all I can do now. I am tired of playing with loaded dice.

Your unfortunate daughter'

Pavani wrote the letter and put it on the table below the paperweight. Seemed something very violent was going on in her mind.

Om was still sitting next to Jaya and he knew that his daughter is strong and would come out of this toughest time but Jaya who was physically, mentally, and emotionally weak and needed his support.

Suddenly, Jaya complained of severe chest pain. She cried out in agony. Before Om could understand anything, she lost consciousness. Om called out to Pavani in panic. Frantically, he rubbed Jaya's hands vigorously and sprinkled some water on her face. Within minutes, Jaya had left the world. She could fight her disease but she could not fight the turbulence of her daughter's life.

Om cried and shouted for Pavani.

Pavani was still looking at the fan and seemed she was firm on her decision. This was the most tragic evening for the family. The happy-go-lucky family had woven many bright and bold dreams for each other. Tonight, the fabric of those dreams was torn rudely into ribbons. Life took everything from them that night.

Chapter - 20

Ms Roy Chaudhary fell silent.

Mrinalini was speechless with shock. She was so involved in the story that she had forgotten to turn off the recorder on her iPad. Ms Roy Chaudhary shook her out of her trance. Mrinalini apologized and immediately turned off the recorder.

She put her iPad in her bag and took out her water bottle to take a sip and compose herself.

"How do you know this story?" she asked Ms Roy Chaudhary.

"I know the girl, Pavani. I have seen her grow up. She is my inspiration for the work I do," replied Ms Roy Chaudhary.

Mrinalini was deep in thought. She was reviewing the story in her mind, thinking of each character. After a moment, she asked hesitantly, "I-I-I do not know but my sixth sense says you are somewhere part of this story."

Ms Roy Choudhary gave her a smile without saying anything. Just then there was an announcement asking the passengers to fasten their seat belts since they were about to land in Delhi.

* * *

When the plane landed at the New Delhi airport, both Ms Roy Chaudhary and Mrinalini collected their baggage and moved out of the plane. They were about to say goodbye to each other when Mrinalini saw Swapna waving to them. Mrinalini looked at her and smiled and waved back. Ms Roy Chaudhary waved to Swapna too.

In the next few seconds, Swapna came over to them and Ms Roy Chaudhary, "How are you, Ms Roy Chaudhary?"

Ms Roy Chaudhary smiled and said, "I am good, Swapna. I am privileged to receive a warm welcome from you. I did not know I was important enough for a famous journalist like you to invest so much attention!"

"One can't always know one's own value, Ms Roy Chaudhary," said Swapna, smiling warmly. "Folks who maintain a low profile and keep on doing their job without fanfare are the real heroes of our country. Rather I would say Sheros of our society. I think they ought to be covered. We all need to be inspired from time to time!"

Turning to Mrinalini she said, "Did you get enough time to interview Ms Roy Chaudhary?"

On receiving an affirmation, both Swapna and Mrinalini thanked Ms Roy Chaudhary profusely for her time and openness and said their goodbyes to her.

* * *

On reaching home, Ms Roy Chaudhary had a quick nap before her phone started ringing around 5 pm. It was one of the assistants at her office who called her excitedly and asked her to turn on one of the news channels.

Intrigued, she tuned into Republic TV Channel. There was breaking news ticker flashing on the screen announced the year's Ramon Magsaysay Award for Emergent leadership. The award was conferred on Ms Roy Chaudhary!

Ms Roy Chaudhary was stunned. She sat down slowly, her mouth agape. The moment turned surreal and dream-like. Frantically, she skimmed through the other channels. It was the same news everywhere! She was so stunned it didn't occur to her to call her out to her father.

A couple of minutes later, her father emerged from his room and knew something was up from her expression. Before he could ask her anything, he noticed the television screen. Disbelief writ large on his face, he sat down next to her. Both father and daughter did not talk to each other but stared wordlessly at the television screen, waiting desperately for the advertisements to get over.

Soon, the advertisements were over and the news started.

"Good Evening! Here is breaking news of this hour. This year's Ramon Magsaysay Award for emergent leadership goes to Ms Roy Chaudhary. She is a well-known name in the NGO fraternity. The award is given to an individual below forty years of age whose efforts have had a major positive impact on society. India is proud of her achievements. Our correspondents are trying to reach her. We will shortly connect with her."

After this, the news anchor moved on to some other news. Ms Roy Chaudhary looked at her father and both hugged each other. They looked delirious with joy!

Within minutes, all the phone in the house began ringing. Congratulatory messages began to pour in on social media. Many news channel correspondents converged outside her society building, wanting to interview her. Knowing she couldn't handle them all individually, she quickly wrote a statement in Hindi and English for the news channels.

Around nine o'clock, she got a call from Swapna who called her to congratulate. She now knew why Mrinalini interviewed her. She wanted to get the entire story before it became difficult for her to get time from her. She was now sure that the next edition of The Times of India would have her entire story. She was still wondering about how she would get such big story coverage in the national newspaper.

Friends and family began dropping in with congratulations. The house had turned into an impromptu party which lasted until dawn. Meanwhile, many residents of her building were happily giving interviews to TV channels for their twenty seconds of reflected glory, telling people what she liked and disliked!

* * *

[29 days before]

Next morning Ms Roy Chaudhary was the first to read the newspaper. She peeked into her father's room; he was not there. She knew he must have gone for his morning walk.

The headline on the front page declared: *Another Magsaysay Award for an Indian*! It covered all the work done by her NGO. It had the same photo which Mrinalini had clicked at the airport. Hurriedly she scanned the cover-story to see if the Pavani story had been given out. It wasn't. She heaved a sigh of relief.

She made a cup of coffee for herself before reading the story in detail. One paragraph towards the end caught her attention.

When asked who had inspired her to begin this work, the article said, *Ms Roy Chaudhary, revealed that she had been inspired by a girl to dedicate herself to bring about this change in society. Happily, Ms Roy Chaudhary was kind enough to tell us all about the girl. Who was that girl and what is her story? We would be happy to share the girl's story in the coming four weeks! Do stay tuned to us!*

Ms Roy Chaudhary could guess what Swapna was planning. She planned to start a buzz around the girl's story!

* * *

For the next four weeks, every day on page seven, a part of Pavani's story was published under the title *'There was a Girl...'* By the end of the week, people had begun sharing it all over social media.

Many people came forward to support her NGO. Funding began to pour in. Her days were super busy. She was rushed off her feet. She was very happy to see that the change which she wanted to bring into society was at last happening.

Everywhere she went, she was asked who that girl was. Many news channels started portraying her as that girl. Folks on social media started asking to reveal the identity of the girl. She refused politely but firmly each time.

* * *

[4 days before]

When Ms Roy Chaudhary landed at Manila airport, she was accompanied by many Indian journalists to cover the award function. Swapna was also among them. In every interaction with a journalist, they asked her who the girl was. Some even asked her if it was her own story. She was fed up with the question!

On award night, Ms Roy Chaudhary wore a magnificent maroon gown sponsored by a top Indian designer. Her gown complemented her tall, lean look and narrow, almost fragile frame.

At 7:00 pm, Ms Roy Chaudhary reached the venue. She was welcomed by the representatives of the trust along with many journalists who had travelled from various countries to cover this event.

It was an opulently decorated area and at venue gate, escorts were standing with plaque card to welcome each awardee. Her escort took her to another room where photo session was planned before the award ceremony. She met with the other awardees over there. Post that, there was a photo session with each of the awardees.

After the photo session, all awardees reached the main function hall. Ms Roy Chaudhary sat in the first row along with the awardees, organizers and VVIPs.

Finally, the moment arrived! Her name was announced to receive the award and say a few words. It was a breath-taking feeling when she stepped up to the dais to receive her award.

She had never dreamt of this moment when she had begun her journey a decade ago. The moment was crammed with myriad sensations. Her commitment to the noble cause, the many ups and downs she had faced in her long and remarkable journey and the things which had inspired her to begin!

Finally, she stepped up to the dais and received her award. The hall erupted into applause. Footlights glaring, cameras whirring, there came a moment when the personal history of one individual stood tall to influence the future of a nation. It was a solemn moment for Ms Roy Chaudhary.

After receiving the award, she was given the microphone. The hall fell silent.

"Good Evening, Ladies and Gentlemen! First, I would like to thank the jury, my fellow Indians and my father for appreciating and supporting my work. I particularly miss my mother today. She would have been delighted with what I have managed to achieve. And I thank you all for your belief in me. I wouldn't have been standing before you today if you had not believed in me! Thank you for your love and support!

"I'd like to share a few snippets from my decade long journey. I began with nothing but a dream and a conviction that the thing I proposed to do would impact many lives. People laugh at you when you share your dreams with them. They discourage and dissuade you and call you mad.

"Dreams, the ones you see with your eyes wide open, are incredibly powerful. They can put in touch with people and resources that would help your cause. They are a fount of ideas and breakthroughs. If we follow it, there is no dream which is difficult to achieve. I wanted to share a few snippets of my decade long journey if organizers permit me to speak for ten minutes."

She looked questioningly at the anchor. Anchor smiled and gave her a thumbs up. Ms Roy Chaudhary smiled and continued.

"India is one of the most diverse countries of the world. It has many different languages, religions and lifestyles. It is difficult to devise one policy which could cover everyone.

"Religions, social classes and castes-all follow the malpractice of dowry. The scourge exists everywhere in different forms. For some people, the amount of dowry they extracted is something to boast about. Some communities have even drawn up rate cards to simplify things. Can you imagine the shame of it? This is what I set out to fight ten years ago.

"Honestly, I had no idea how to go about it. After much deliberation, I realized that the real categorization is not on the basis of caste, creed or religion. The actual lines of demarcation were much simpler. There are just two kinds of people in our society-those who drive malpractices like dowry and those who are being driven by those people. I saw no way to bring about a change in the former category, so I decided to see how I could influence the latter.

"I took the help of some friends and interviewed many young men, all progressive thinkers. Some were married some were on the verge of tying the knot. We asked them why they were not able to oppose their parents when they demanded dowry.

"We found that young men do not oppose their parents because of the money their parents have invested toward their upbringing and education. This investment brings them to the level where they can sustain themselves. When parents of a young man demand dowry he cannot protest because he is under a financial and moral obligation to them. Many boys we interviewed broke down because they felt tied in a bind that they couldn't escape. Some were very bitter too, likening their parents' greed to the avarice of Shylock who insisted on his pound of flesh.

"We found a way to break this stranglehold when a few of our interviewees fervently declared that they wouldn't have submitted to their parents' demand for dowry if they had found some other means of funding their education. They would have been independent and could have convinced their parents.

"The road ahead was clear. We had to find a way to finance the higher education of boys. Their parents would only pay the first fee instalment and we would finance the rest as a loan. At the time of signing the loan documents, we took a written undertaking from both, the student and his parents, that they would not demand a dowry when the boy gets married.

"Since the loan repayment duration would be several years after their course was over, we had a way to monitor if they kept their promise or not. If we found that they had defaulted on their promise and had taken a dowry, they would have to pay a heavy penalty in the form of higher interest on the loan amount.

"I am happy to say, though, that in last one decade not a single borrower has defaulted on his promise. Now past beneficiaries have begun supporting us by helping us spread the word and also by contributing financially. We supported them and now they are supporting us!

"If you look at it, what is happening to our all government funded colleges or institutes? All these institutes are funded by the government who subsidise the fee and these government funded students later becomes a mine of money laundering.

"Why can't we make all colleges at par so there is no subsidised fee in any institutes? Be it government or private. Let the students with their parents take the additional funding from government monitored agencies so that we can control this malpractice."

"To help this further, the government can make a law to say that anyone who takes dowry will not be entitled to any government schemes or jobs. In addition, they will be asked to compensate the government for the subsidized fee by paying the full, unsubsidized fee for the course they attended. The burden of the unsubsidized fee would be penalty enough for them.

"Lastly, I must talk about the story of the girl who inspired me to do what I have done. My journalist friends have been asking me to reveal the identity of that girl. So today I am revealing it.

"Pavani is a pseudonym. It is my own story that I narrated to the journalist who interviewed me!"

She had to pause. The auditorium gasped and fell silent, then burst into deafening applause! She stood under the footlights, her head bowed and eyes misty, as the audience got to their feet and gave her a standing ovation amidst cries of *Bravo* and *Well Done!*

She waited for the applause to end and people to resume their seats before she resumed, a solemn smile lighting up her face.

"As I stand here today, I find only gratitude in my heart for all those who helped me in this journey. I thank those who created the crisis that made me tough enough to begin this journey. I bear no grudges. You are where you are because of the decisions you took yesterday and today's moves will decide where you will be tomorrow!

"I reacted positively to what life threw at me and I am happy that I could make difference. I thank Swapna for giving wings to my story. It seems to have connected with people and is being discussed all over the country. I hope it inspires other people. If all the girls decide that they will not marry anyone who demands dowry, we can solve this issue much quicker. Parents of boys cannot keep their sons unmarried forever!

"With this, I thank all of you for your support, patient listening and blessings!"

Ms Roy Chaudhary was emotional as she walked down from dais with the award in her hand. The audience cheered her all the way to her seat.

* * *

[1 day before]

When Ms Roy Chaudhary returned from the Philippines, she was welcomed by her entire staff. A large group of journalists converged upon her, asking questions. She waved her hand to them and vanished in the midst of her team.

Epilogue

It is a lovely, cloudy morning when Ms Roy Chaudhary got up. She accompanied her father for their morning walk. They returned home in half an hour and she was having her tea when her mobile phone rang. The screen displayed a private number.

She picked the phone and said, "Hello!"

"Hello, is it Ms Roy Chaudhary?" said a male voice.

"Yes, Ms Roy Chaudhary speaking!" she replied.

"Hi, Ms Roy Chaudhary, this is K P Singh speaking from PMO!" said the voice solemnly.

Ms Roy Chaudhary is astonished. She does not know how to react and is a little flustered.

"Yes, Mr Singh. How can I help you?" she said, her pulse racing.

"Mr Prime Minister wants to talk to you," said the voice curtly.

"Really!?"

"Give me thirty seconds to connect you," said the voice woodenly.

Feeling surreal, Ms Roy Chaudhary looked at her phone as the hold music began to blare. It was playing the instrumental of the famous song *'Saare Jahan se Achchha, Hindustan Hamara'*. After a few seconds, background music stopped and a well-known, commanding voice came on.

"Hello, Ms Roy Chaudhary, heartiest congratulations for your great work and recognition!"

Ms Roy Chaudhary was dumbstruck. She tried to collect her wits and said, "H-H-Hello sir. Thanks a lot for your kind wishes! It is my honour to get a call from our Prime Minister on my achievements! I am speechless, sir!"

"No Ms Roy Chaudhary. You should not be speechless. Now it the time for you to speak."

"I'm sorry, sir? I could not get you."

"I heard your televised speech yesterday. Each word you said was true. We have become a nation of takers. We want to use all the resources the country offers but don't want to give anything back to it. We don't care about creating a better society either.

"I really liked your idea. I have discussed it with some of my senior colleagues and we all are aligned with your thought process. We are planning to set up a team to draft a new policy and implement it across India. It would be great if you would join our team to motivate and guide so that we take the right steps and build the nation which is free of the evil of dowry. Tell me, will you join us?"

"Sir, I don't have words to thank you, sir!" said Ms Roy Chaudhary with earnest delight. "It would be an honour to join. Thanks for implementing this on the national level."

"Please don't say thanks! I thank you for devoting your entire life for this excellent cause. Thank you for not letting your history stop you from building a fantastic future not only for yourself but for many others! We need more people like you to come forward with ideas for nation building!"

"Sir, I have no words to tell you what your words mean to me. Thank you!" said she, overwhelmed and nearly in tears.

"So can we meet today for lunch?" the PM asked.

"Sure, sir!" she replied, with a gasp of happiness!

"So see you at 1:00 pm at my residence. You will get a call from my office for logistics," he said.

"Okay, sir!" responded Ms Roy Chaudhary.

The call disconnected and Ms Roy Chaudhary jumped up to announce the happy news to her father!

Acknowledgements

After publishing my first book '3D of Life: 3D (Dimensions) of Life (Love, Support and Sacrifice)', I was looking for a subject that touches millions and later after having many discussions with my near and dear, I thought to create my fiction world around any malpractices of the society. I am thankful to my friends who gave their precious time to finalise a topic on which I can further work on. Thank you all for your time and getting into nitty-gritty of the topics and discussing with me some vague ideas as well.

I would like to thank my wife Deepti and my sons Tanay and Tejas for their support and best wishes. A big thank you to all who have played a vital role in my life as I consider everyone as my teacher.

Special thanks to Pooja, Priya and Richa for proofreading the first draft of this book. Your inputs have been very valuable and instrumental in the making of this book.

My special thanks to my Editor who has done a fantastic job and GenNext Publication for publishing this book.

Other book by the author

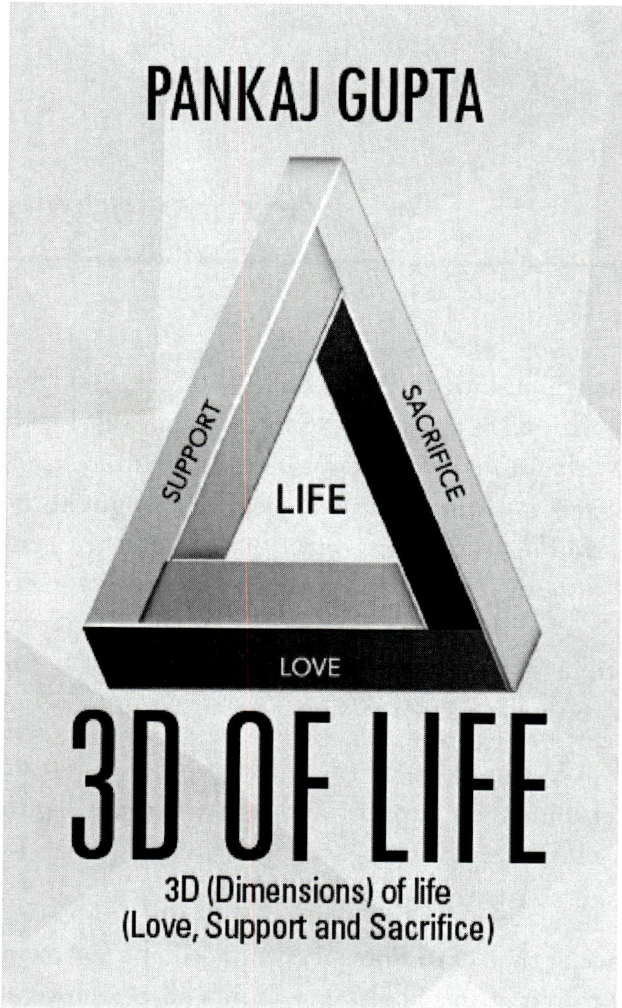